D0371869

DATE DUE AUG 0 5

GAYLORD			PRINTED IN U.S.A.

BRINGING UP THE BONES

LARA M. ZEISES

BRINGING UP THE BONES

DELACORTE PRESS

Published by
Delacorte Press
an imprint of
Random House Children's Books
a division of Random House, Inc.
1540 Broadway
New York, New York 10036

Visit us on the Web! www.randomhouse.com/teens
Educators and librarians, for a variety of teaching tools, visit us at
www.randomhouse.com/teachers

Cataloging-in-Publication Data is available from the Library of Congress.

ISBN 0-385-73001-2

The text of this book is set in 11-point Berkeley Book.

Book design by Saho Fujii

Manufactured in the United States of America

October 2002

10 9 8 7 6 5 4 3 2 1

BVG

To BJM,
for lessons learned

ACKNOWLEDGMENTS

FIRST AND FOREMOST, I am grateful for all of the wonderful teachers I've been lucky enough to encounter over the years, especially Cruce Stark, for being the first adult to ever take my writing seriously; Lisa Jahn-Clough, for her continued support and friendship, and for giving me a first-class passport into the world of children's writing; Andre Dubus III, for teaching me about pathos, pity, and Art (capital A intended); and Myra McLarey, for believing in this story—and for helping me believe in myself.

TO THE MANY EDITORS at Random House Children's Books who make up the judging committee for the Delacorte Press Prize for a First Young Adult Novel, I thank you for taking a chance on me and my little book. I'm also thankful for my editor, Diana Capriotti, who guided me through the revision process with admirable grace and patience.

I FEEL LUCKY to have known so many talented people who freely gave their time to offer me feedback at various stages, including Mark Adam, Tiffany Benduhn, Kate Cook, Marla Feuerstein, Allison Monro, and Rachel Moulton. I am especially indebted to fellow Emersonians Laurie Stolarz and Steven Goldman; their thoughtful critiques, endless encouragement, and enviable talent have not only inspired me, but have also made me a stronger writer.

A BIG SLOPPY KISS goes out to Pamela at Calder Publications and Dr. Edison Amos at Sword and Stone, for granting my permission requests quickly and cheaply.

LAST, BUT NEVER LEAST, I want to express my love and gratitude to some of the members of my korass: Andrew Charnik, for believing in an always; Bec Schmidt, for understanding and never judging; Nancy Weinstein, for helping me find the way; the Magnusons, for making me an honorary member of their family; the Rosens (who really *are* my family!), for always coming through for me; and Mary Cotillo, my unofficial editor, for shrinking the tallest of hurdles, and for making me laugh even when I feel like crying.

the hours after you are gone are so leaden
they will always start dragging too soon
the grapples clawing blindly the bed of want
bringing up the bones the old loves
sockets filled once with eyes like yours
all always is it better too soon than never
the black want splashing their faces
saying again nine days never floated the loved
nor nine months
nor nine lives

—from *Cascando* by Samuel Beckett

PROLOGUE

IT CAME ON THE SATURDAY BEFORE MIDTERMS, a piece of college-ruled paper crammed into a small, plain white envelope. There was no return address, but I saw the California postmark and knew it was from Benji. *Bridget,* it began. Not *Dear Bridget,* mind you. Just my name, followed by a colon. Like a memo. A breakup memo.

> *Bridget:*
>
> *This is my third attempt to write this letter. I don't know what to say except I'm sorry. I've tried to love you as much as you say you love me but the truth is I don't think I do. You know me better than any other person on the planet but it's still not enough. I don't think love can be reduced to an equation. Friendship + Attraction ≠ Love. I wish we could go back to being*

just friends but I'm not sure that's possible. Please
don't call me or write me or try to change my mind.
It will only make things hurt more.

—Benji

Benji never really wanted to be my boyfriend, just my best friend, but I loved him from the first time I saw him, and I didn't know how to stop. So after seven years of best-friendship and seven months of outright begging, he reluctantly gave in and agreed to a trial relationship.

Our official couplehood lasted roughly nine months, until he sent that memo. Geographically, the relationship filled no more than a summer, eleven humid weeks before he put three thousand miles between us. During that time, we made love only once, in the basement of his parents' house the night before he left for school.

We did it quietly, on a warm pile of his laundry that hadn't been packed yet. It wasn't planned, and every elaborate seduction I had ever plotted for the two of us could not compare to the exquisite simplicity of what actually happened.

"I do love you," he whispered as he brushed a stray sock from my breast. "Didn't know love before you."

I kissed him then, pressed his bare chest against my own so tightly a speck of lint couldn't have fit between the two of us. Later, as I watched him sleep, breathing in and out, I tried to imagine feeling any closer to him than I did at that moment, but it simply wasn't possible. We had become one person, Benji and me. Two old souls destined to die in each other's arms.

Except, of course, Benji died alone.

ONE

MY NAME IS BRIDGET EDELSTEIN. I am eighteen years old and I have never felt more alone in my entire life.

This isn't the fault of the people in my world, who've tried their hardest to make me believe things will be "normal" sometime in the future. There's Ellie, my best girlfriend, who has appointed herself director of my well-being (i.e., brings me back issues of *People,* cartons of Camel Lights, and countless pints of Ben & Jerry's New York Super Fudge Chunk). There's my stepfather, Fitzi, who spent the summer dragging me to Blue Rocks ball games, pumping me full of fried foods at O'Friel's, and slipping me sizable wads of cash to help subsidize the tiny studio apartment I moved into a few weeks after my high school graduation. Even my mother, who didn't bother to come to the funeral, routinely sends me touchy-feely self-help books with titles like *You're Gone, But I'm Still Here* that her manicurist "highly recommends."

But there's only so long you can endure the practiced pity looks, the soft "How *are* you?" tone of voice, before you want to run screaming into a closet with a lock on the inside. How am I? I'm ready to explode, but too exhausted to actually do it.

I've tried to maintain a veneer of normalcy. I get up, I go to work, I go to bed. I'll shoot some pool with Fitzi or go to the movies with Ellie, and I'll have a good time, maybe even laugh a little. But there's always a trigger—I'll hear a snippet of one of our songs on the radio or the squeal of a hard brake at a stoplight and my insides float out until I'm sort of hovering over the scene. *Watching* myself instead of being myself. Ellie thinks it's guilt, that I'm okay until I start having too much fun and then I suddenly remember I'm supposed to be morbidly depressed, so I make myself go cold. But it's not like that. I don't feel bad when I laugh. I think it's them. The others. I'll laugh and I'll feel them tense up, as if they're bracing themselves for what's to follow. It makes me self-conscious, and that's why I stop.

"You need time," my therapist routinely tells me at our weekly sessions that Fitzi's been funding since last August.

But it's been nearly seven months since Benji died and I still dream of him nightly. Sometimes they are good dreams, smelling of salt water, like the hot summer afternoons spent down on the beach, where Benji would school me in East Coast sea nettles as we walked along the seaweed-strewn

6

shore. Other times they play more like newsreels of events I've simply forgotten.

I am already beginning to forget.

Time—that was Benji's parting gift to me. Just before he boarded the plane for California, he pressed a small spice jar of thyme into my palm. In my ear he whispered, "If I could save time in a bottle," and I thought it was a joke until I turned and saw his face, devoid of all humor. His eyes caught mine then, held them captive in the kind of silent conversation you can have only with someone who knows you better than you know yourself. Then a disembodied voice called for rows eighteen and up, and the moment was lost. Benji clapped his hands and said, "Well, Bridge, that's me," and after a perfunctory, decidedly unromantic peck on my cheek, he disappeared into the plane, never once looking back.

It happened last February, the day before Valentine's Day, around six A.M. From what we can piece together, Benji was driving home from a volunteer gig at a preserved beach just north of Arcata, where he had spent the night rescuing sea turtle eggs, or doing something equally noble. An eighteen-wheeler slammed into the side of his Buick. The force of the collision sent his car across two lanes, over a flimsy guardrail, and down a steep ravine. Police said it was a freak accident, that the driver had had a heart attack—no trace of drugs or alcohol in his blood. Doctors said Benji didn't suffer, that the fall snapped his neck and he was dead long before the car hit the ground. As if these things are supposed to bring us comfort.

He's still dead, after all.

The viewing turned into a mini high school reunion. They all came out to say goodbye to Benji: the marching band, the soccer team, the drama brats—kids who'd gone to college three states away managed to make it home for the social event of the season. Even Mr. Hirsch, the crusty geometry teacher who never seemed to like any of his pupils—except Benji, of course—even he put in an appearance.

Over the objections of Benji's father, Mr. Gilbert, who for some unknown reason has never liked me, Benji's mother asked me to join them in the receiving line. Face after face passed before me. Half of them I couldn't put a name to. But people hugged me, cried to me, tried to console me with empty words and false promises—Benji is in a better place now. This was meant to be.

I didn't cry then, not to those people, blind sheep who believed Benji was watching over us from some mythical kingdom. I knew better. I knew that all that was left was his corpse, today resting in a satin-lined coffin, tomorrow being fed to an incinerator and then dumped into a big brass urn. People marveled at my strength, admired the brave front I put forth—for their sake, they assumed. I let them believe this, mostly because I was too tired to explain what I was really feeling.

Anna, Benji's fourteen-year-old sister, clutched my hand

tightly enough to cut off the circulation. She couldn't stop sobbing, choking on the sadness that spread like cancer throughout the congregation of Benji's family and friends. I wished I could be like her, but instead, I waited until I was left alone with him, until I could expose my personal grief privately.

I was one of the last to look at Benji's body. I had never seen a dead person before. My mom's dad had died when I was still a baby; my father's father was Jewish and we had followed the tradition of a closed-casket funeral. So there was no way I could've been prepared for this lifeless Benji, a wax dummy of a body with too-dark skin and too-neat hair.

His eyes were closed, and all I could think was that I wanted to see those eyes one last time. Gingerly, I reached forward, put my thumb on his left eyelid. The flesh had a rubbery feel and the lid wouldn't move. I leaned closer, tugging at the eye. That's when I realized it had been sealed shut. A great big claw clutched at my lungs, stole my breath. But I stayed with him, carefully slipped a lock of my hair into the webbing between his thumb and pointer finger. Then I kissed him, flat on the mouth. His lips didn't just look like wax. They *were* wax. Reconstructed lips for a poorly reconstructed face.

"Bridget," Mr. Gilbert called to me from across the room. "It's time to go." His voice, a blackboard scratch across so much silence, gave me goose bumps. I turned toward him slowly, not knowing how much he had seen. He didn't say anything else, just looked at me, his thin mouth puckered, his wide-arching eyebrows pulled tightly into the bridge of his nose.

"Coming," I said. He nodded, then just stood there. Waiting. I slid past him into the lobby, where Mrs. Gilbert's marshmallow arms welcomed me. I clung to her, hoping the pain would disappear in the thick folds of her flesh.

There's a large fireproof lockbox at the bottom of my closet, filled with letters and photographs and journals and ticket stubs—documentation spanning our entire relationship. Proof that there was once a life with Benji, as opposed to the loneliness I have now. And yet I can't completely shake the feeling that none of it was real, or maybe that it wasn't real enough. I remember the important moments with complete clarity—it's the little things that are slipping away. Peanut, for example—what was Peanut? Once upon a time it was a nickname for someone, or something. Now it's just a word. I can't count the number of nights I've been unable to fall asleep, trying to open the right file in my memory. I've become obsessed. Which classmate's car did we christen Peanut? Whose homecoming date?

Eventually I'll fall asleep, and I'll forget for a few days that I've lost the significance of Peanut. But then I'll remember something else that's been lost, and the cycle will start all over again.

I know that in the grand scheme of things, Peanut plays a minuscule part. I guess before, it wouldn't have mattered much. Before, when there were an infinite number of opportunities to create Peanut replacements. But there will be no new nicknames now, no new inside jokes, no new memories—no new anything. So in a way, Peanut is all I have left.

TWO

THESE ARE SOME OF THE WAYS my life has changed since Benji died:

1. I DON'T GIVE A SHIT ABOUT GOING TO COLLEGE.
2. I WILL DRIVE TWENTY MILES OUT OF MY WAY TO AVOID MAJOR HIGHWAYS.
3. I CAN'T LISTEN TO MY TORI AMOS CDS ANYMORE.
4. I SEE A THERAPIST ONCE A WEEK.
5. BLACK SWEATPANTS HAVE BECOME MY UNOFFICIAL UNIFORM.

This is just a partial list. I'd probably need five notebooks to include everything that's different now.

Ellie thinks I haven't noticed how I've changed, but I'm not completely oblivious. I've never been one-hundred-percent, rock-solid stable, but when I lost Benji, it was as if my internal motor went kaput. Now stupid little things like brushing my teeth before bed totally sap my energy. And handling Ellie is like flossing after every single bite of food.

At least once a week, Ellie stops by with a plate of baked goods, like a pixie version of my grandma Sadie. She calls my tiny apartment the Cave, mostly because I'm not a huge fan of natural light and use low-wattage bulbs in the few lamps I possess. So Ellie's first order of business is to pull up the shades. Then, as my eyes water from the sudden brightness, she begins her inspection. Her sharp brown eyes scan the floor, taking a mental tally of how much laundry I've let accumulate there. Then she moves to the glass collection— "When was the last time you did dishes, Bridge? Fourth of July?"—and homes in on the back wall of my bedroom-slash-living room, on the arrangement of framed photos I've hung: Benji in his Superman T-shirt, spinning devilishly on a kiddie-park merry-go-round. Benji buried neck-deep in sand, wearing a plastic bucket on his head. Benji sprawled on his parents' green-and-gold plaid sofa, sleeping peacefully under a pilfered airline blanket.

These she never comments on, just drinks in. I can see the gears of her mind churning away on each visit, trying to find the perfect words with which to tell me exactly how loony she thinks I've become. But something makes her hold her tongue. Her restraint is often the only thing that keeps me from telling her to get lost.

Today's visit is unexpected; Ellie's manager at the Food-n-

Stuff rarely gives her Friday afternoons off. After she's made the rounds, she stands in front of the photo wall and says, "I want you to do me a favor."

"Sure," I say. "What?"

Ellie breathes deeply. "I want you to take some of these down."

"Why?"

"Because I don't think they're healthy."

I decide to play innocent, and keeping my eyes locked on Ellie's, say, "Pictures are bad?"

"You know what I mean, Bridge," she says. "It's like a shrine in here."

I sit on the edge of the bed and survey the wall. My fingers toy with the frayed elastic cuff of my sweatpants and I try to blink Ellie away.

It doesn't work.

She sits beside me. "I'm worried about you."

"I'm fine."

Ellie gives me one of those looks. "How long have we known each other? Nine years?"

"Then you should know by now lectures don't work on me."

She drops her hand onto my knee. "I know it's hard. It was hard on all of us. He was my friend, too."

"It's not the same," I say.

"Well, no, but—"

"What do you want me to do? Forget I ever knew him?"

Ellie sighs then, a familiar, exasperated sigh. "No." She

runs her tongue over a sparkly-lipsticked lip. "But this isn't good. I mean, you have to get past this."

I hate the way she says that. As if I'm moping over a bad date, or a guinea pig that has suddenly gone to disposable-pet heaven. Benji *wasn't* disposable. He wasn't replaceable or forgettable, either. I feel hot anger rush to my cheeks, and in a flash I am off the bed and at the wall. I rip off the center-piece—Benji's senior portrait—and toss it onto a nearby pile of laundry.

"There," I say. "Is that better?" Ellie's left eye twitches slightly. I take a deep breath and smooth some stray curls off my face. "Look, I know you want to help, but I don't think pictures are the problem."

"What does your therapist say?"

My body tenses at the word. I'm not completely comfort-able with the idea of going to a shrink, let alone having Ellie ask about the awkward sessions in such a casual way. I shrug and look away.

"Listen," Ellie says. "I need another favor. I met this guy Marcus last week, at Rainbow Records. Totally delish. Any-way, he and his roommates are throwing a party tonight, and I want you to come with me."

Her request catches me so completely off guard that I can't even think of a plausible lie, like I can't go because I'm scheduled to work or something. Ellie must sense my vul-nerability, because she goes in for the kill: "You can't say no, Bridget. You know I haven't asked you to do something like this in ages, and I wouldn't ask you now except for the fact

15

that this guy is so perfect—completely obsessed with Jeff Buckley *and* James Brown—and how often do you find a guy like that? Plus, this would be so good for you. I mean *so* good. Please say yes, please please *please*."

"Okay," I say, more to shut her up than anything. Besides, I think, I can probably worm out of it later.

"Yay!" Ellie squeals, throwing her arms around me. "Oh, Bridge, it's going to be so much fun, I promise."

She tells me she'll pick me up at nine and I should wear anything that isn't black. Then, to my relief, she says she has to run. With a quick kiss on my cheek, she's off.

I look out the window, watching Ellie's black Nissan zip out the driveway and onto the main road. I wait until the car has disappeared before rehanging the portrait. Benji, clad in a pearl-gray suit and cherry bow tie, grins at me from the wall.

Benji's graduation night, exactly one year before my own. The weather was gross; hot, sticky air coated my skin, made my daisy-print sundress feel damp and moldy. Ellie and I sat in the football stadium's bleachers with the Gilberts, listening to the marching band bleating its stirring rendition of "The Halls of Haley High," our cheesy school song. Giggling as its finale was cut short when the brass section launched into "Road to Nowhere"—an homage to Benji, led by his trumpet-blowing buddy, Jack. Watching Benji, who saluted me from the platform with his left hand, clutching his newly earned diploma in the other.

After the ceremony we all headed to the Gilberts' house

for a modest Food-n-Stuff–catered reception. When all his family obligations had been met, Benji gave the signal and a whole group of us—me; Ellie; Jack; Jack's girlfriend, Echo; this guy from Benji's class who I knew only as Action Dan— loaded into the Gilbert family van and took off. We had scrounged up some camping gear and we drove the fifteen miles south to Lums Pond. As Jack and Action Dan wrestled with the tents, Ellie and I took up a collection, then headed to a nearby Wawa to stock up on Spam, Ball Park franks, and Yoo-Hoo. When we returned, Benji was jumping around in front of the cook pit, bellowing, "Behold, Bendor, lord of fire." The orange flames cast a half-crazed look on his face, and he looked so good, I wanted to rip off his Superman T-shirt and jump his bones right then and there. Friendship was not satisfying me by a long shot.

Instead, I waited patiently, blackening hot dogs in the raging fire, listening to him and Jack and Action Dan reminisce, laughing in all the right places. Finally, they retreated to their respective tents. Benji lagged behind, poking a dead branch into the smoldering embers. I crept up behind him, wrapped my arms around his chest, and rested my chin on his shoulder.

"Pretty night," I said. "Wanna sleep outside?"

Benji nodded, using his stick to draw swirls in the pile of ash. "Yeah, okay."

We dragged our sleeping bags about a dozen feet from the tents. Ever the gentleman, Benji cleared my space of knotty wood and pebbles.

"Here you are, Miss Bridget," he said, sweeping his arm and bowing deeply. "I hope you find the accommodations to your satisfaction."

"Indeed, I think I shall."

Despite the still-oppressive heat, Benji climbed into his bag, curling his arm into a makeshift pillow. "Night," he said, closing his eyes.

I stood for a second, watching over him, wondering how to make my move. In the end, I simply let my body go slack and slipped as gracefully as possible to the ground next to him. Benji grumbled, "Whaddya want?"

"You," I said.

He laughed, a short, sharp laugh. "Oh, puh-leeze," he said, swatting me away. "You insult me with your uninspired pickup line. Try again."

Shedding all inhibition, I snaked up his back, letting my lips graze the outer rim of his ear. "What would you say if I offered to make a man of you, right here, right now?"

Without skipping a beat, he said, "Haven't we been through this?"

"Benji," I moaned, flopping over on my stomach. "Why won't you let me?"

"Let you what? Fuck me in the middle of a shitty state park?" He rolled onto his other side, so that he was facing me. "Bridget—no."

Irritated, I sat up. "I don't want to . . . *fuck* you," I said.

"Well, what *do* you want?"

"I want to lie here next to you until morning. Wake up with you still here."

Benji snorted. "When did I become Fabio?"

"Look, you," I said. "You can act like there's nothing between us, but we both know I've never been just your friend. I'm more than a girlfriend, even though you can't admit it. I'm your soul mate, you schmuck, and it's about time our souls actually started mating."

"Now?" he said, wriggling out of his waterproof cocoon. "I'm leaving in three months."

"Well, yeah. And who knows—I may never see you again."

"Oh, I don't know about that."

"Face it, B-man. Fleeing to a school three thousand miles away . . . You don't go that far unless you're getting away from something. Something you won't be all that anxious to return to."

His face softened. "Not you. I'm not fleeing you."

"Doesn't matter." I pouted. "You're still leaving."

In a rare moment of tenderness, Benji scooted closer, wrapped his hands around mine. "You *will* see me again."

I lifted my face, let my eyes latch on to his. "Kiss me," I said plainly, simply. "Can you do that?"

We sat silent, frozen in a moment that felt like a millennium, years of friendship and sexual tension bubbling between us. Then, in one swift move, his clammy hand shot up and drew me to him. He tasted like marshmallow-covered Spam, but I didn't care. I'd never been kissed like this before. His mouth, suddenly hungry, devoured my own. My stomach felt like it did after the first sip of steaming soup on a frigid day, and I melted into him until I could feel the *thump-thump* of his heart against mine. *Finally*. This wasn't kissing for kissing's sake. This was raw, lip-bruising Kissing with a capital *K*. Benji kissed me breathless to the score of a cicada symphony, kissed me until I lost track of which mouth belonged to whom, kissed me until I collapsed on top of him in a blissful, dizzy heap.

I stare at the blown-up snapshot on my wall, the lines of Benji's face melting like hot crayon, the colors swirling together in a van Gogh blur. The blue of his eyes running like wet ink into the pinky-peach flesh of his face, smashing into a sideburn beach of sun-streaked hair.

His *hair*. So fine and straight and soft and always smelling like the rinds of overripe lemons.

I turn away.

THREE

DESPITE MY INTENTIONS, I never do get around to inventing an excuse for skipping Marcus's party. Besides, maybe Ellie's right. Maybe it will be good for me to get out of the Cave for a while. With the exception of serving people in my capacity as a truck-stop waitress, I have very little social interaction these days.

So around eight, I hop into the shower, scrub off about three days' worth of grime, and in a completely random move, shave my legs. It's been so long since I've done it that the skin hiding underneath all that hair feels too pink and tender to go unmoisturized, so I slather on a thick coat of cocoa butter. Out comes the hair dryer, which is covered in a film of dust. I roll a section of hair around a large-barreled brush and blow the strands smooth.

My hair is the color of fresh-grated cinnamon, or at least

that's what Fitzi tells me. Most people assume this is a gift from Katharine, my Irish mother, and not the bottle of Nice 'n Easy #110 I apply religiously each month. Once we started dating, Benji confessed that after my mouth, he loved my hair best—especially the color, which he said reminded him of Ann-Margret in *Viva Las Vegas*. I've always liked the comparison, but more than that, I liked the look Benji gave me when he'd twist a thick curl around his paddle-shaped thumb.

Since I've gone all out with my hair, I decide to do the makeup thing too. My liquid foundation is so old the pigment has separated from the oil, and it smells a bit like rotten egg. As I begin to sponge some of the vile goop onto my skin, something stops me. It's my face. I must look at it at least twice a day, but at this moment, the girl in the mirror is a stranger to me. My cheeks, once a bit fleshy, have thinned considerably. How? When? They are angular now, skin stretched over bones to form sharp planes and darkened hollows. It's amazing how quickly you can forget there's an actual body housing your brain.

A quick sweep of mascara and a touch of lip gloss complete my low-rent look, and then it's off to wardrobe. I paw through my closet, looking for a decent shirt I can pair with jeans. I find a clingy button-down with three-quarter sleeves that will do the trick, but I'm hesitant as it is black and I'm not sure I can take another one of Ellie's disapproving looks. A quick time check reveals that it's already 8:58; the black shirt wins by default.

Ellie is late, which is nothing new, but sitting on the edge of my futon watching the clock sets my nerves on edge. What am I doing? Going to some faux–frat house beer bash so Ellie can hook up with the next flavor of the month? I am thinking about calling Ellie's cell phone—trying to head her off before she reaches my apartment—when the doorbell rings.

"Look at you," Ellie says when I greet her. She nods in appreciation. "I thought I'd never get you out of those ratty sweatpants."

Before she can deliver another backhanded compliment, and before I can chicken out, I lock the door and we are on our way.

The party, it turns out, is being held on Madison Avenue in a trashy town-home complex not far from Del U's main campus, only a twenty-minute walk from my place. Music thumps against the basement's brick walls, providing a driving bass line for the blur of braying voices whizzing around me. I sit cross-legged in a well-worn Archie Bunker chair, watching a crush of people jimmy their way across the room. Ellie handed me a beer when we first arrived two hours ago, whereupon she promptly abandoned me for the aforementioned Marcus, who wanted her to listen to some Elliot Smith album on his new headphones. I've been in the chair ever since.

I am invisible in my chair. I am eyes peering out from nothingness. My ears ache from the constant noise; my jaw is tired from holding its constant clench. The air is thick with fruity hair spray, Drakkar Noir, and malt liquor. The combination is making me queasy. I think I've served my time.

With a soft grunt, I yank myself out of the chair and gradually push my way to the stairs, a narrow passage congested with two broad-shouldered football players and a couple of stray stoners passing a beer-can bong. Navigating the upstairs living room proves equally precarious; I push through more and more bodies, not sure how I'm supposed to find Ellie in this mess.

She eventually turns up in the bathroom line. "There you are!" Ellie says, a little too bright and a little too loud. "I've been looking all over for you!" I see a smudge of seashell-pink lip gloss on the side of her mouth and notice that the artfully messy bed-head look she created for this evening's festivities now looks decidedly natural. So much for sisterhood.

"I think I'm gonna take off," I say.

"What? It's not even midnight. And how are you getting home?"

"I'm really tired," I fib. "And it's a short walk. I'll see you later, okay?"

Despite Ellie's half-drunken protests, I snake my way through the living room, keeping my eyes on the brass knob of the front door. When I reach it, I feel as though I've just run a medal-worthy obstacle course.

That's when I see him. Sitting alone, sprawled boylike on

the front stoop, his curly hair swooshing about on a gentle breeze. I smell him in almost the same second, a curious combination of maple leaves and wet mulch, kind of like a dewy fall morning in Vermont. It's the smell that makes me linger. I spy a box of Camels parked next to him. I clear my throat and say, "Spare a smoke?"

He turns slightly, looks at me over his right shoulder, his eyes landing on my mouth. Without breaking his gaze, he lifts the pack and hands it to me. Our fingers touch, producing the kind of static electric jolt that makes you think of soap opera love. I barely slip the cig between my lips and he's up, sparking his Zippo. I needlessly cup my hand around the flame, letting my fingers graze his again. "Thanks."

He clicks the lighter shut, his eyes still glued to my mouth. I take advantage of this preoccupation by looking him over. He's taller than me, but not by too terribly much; maybe five-nine or so. Lean build, like a soccer player, with the sweetest dimple between his bottom lip and chin, a small dent just begging to be kissed. The thought makes me blush, or maybe it's the beer. "See you around," I say.

"Think I can have those back?" he asks, his rich voice spurring my face to flame deeper. When I don't answer, he reaches forward and gently tugs his Camels from my hand.

"Oh, right. Sorry about that."

He grins. More dimples, this time in his cheeks. I can't help smiling back.

"So where are you headed?"

"Blair Street."

"Where are you parked?"

"I'm not," I say. "I came with a friend. She wants to stick around, so I figured I'd hoof it."

He nods solemnly. "That's pretty far. You really shouldn't be walking alone this late."

"I'll be fine."

"I have a truck," he says. "Not here—it's parked by North Central. We could walk over there together, and I could give you a ride."

"You don't have to—"

"I want to," he cuts in, giving me another glimpse of that grin.

And so we walk.

We stroll along in silence, climb the stairs to the walkway that stretches over South College. Inside the brick structure, he reaches for my wrist. I stop, let him press me up against a tinted-glass pane. Our mouths smash together with an intensity I haven't felt since that night at Lums Pond. His kiss is like the first drag off a fresh cigarette: hot, spicy, comforting.

We walk more quickly now, past the sprawling brick library, over the lush green mall, past the lot where his truck is parked. My heart beats to the irregular rhythm of his jangling keys. I let this nameless boy rest his hand between my shoulder blades, all the while thinking, *What am I doing? What am I doing?* He fumbles with the electronic pass card at the back door of his dorm, and there are more stairs, and then we're there, at his room, and the sound of his key entering the lock stirs the circus in my stomach.

We go in.

He locks the door behind us. He neglects to turn on a light. My lips are drawn to his like a magnet to metal. We remove each other's clothes at a frenetic pace, the thumping music still ringing in my ears. The wet-mulch smell I noticed earlier intensifies as we wrestle on the thin mattress of his extra-long bed. His lips brush from my breasts to my belly button to the dampened cotton crotch of my panties, which soon find their way to the floor. I come quickly, guiltily. But it doesn't stop there.

He reaches over me to the wood-laminate nightstand, fishes around the top drawer until he finds a condom. I can feel him looking at me in the darkness, can feel him wondering if I'm one of those girls who likes to slip it on the guy herself. My nails dig into the soft flesh of his shoulders; my tongue thrusts itself into his mouth. He decides to do it himself, rolls away from me a bit.

And then he's inside me, and I'm expecting to feel the searing pain I did with Benji but it's not like that this time. Our bodies fit together like puzzle pieces. We rock together, and I feel a trickle of his sweat land on my cheek, and the intimacy of this makes my breath disappear.

I come again.

Now it's his turn. He drives deeper inside me, panting

hard, moaning hard, whimpering as if he were in pain. He finishes with a final yowl, pulls out, and sits back on his legs.

When it is over, I start to cry. Quietly at first, then louder. He says, "Hey, are you okay?" Touches my shoulder gently, but now his hand feels wet and slimy. A slug hand. I brush it away.

"I have a boyfriend," I say, and even as the words escape my lips, I can feel their wrongness. "Had," I correct myself. "I had a boyfriend."

"So which one is it?"

"I'm sorry," I say, still crying. "I'm so sorry."

It takes a couple of beats to register. "Shit."

He sighs deeply, crawls over my legs and out of the bed. Pulls on his clothes as I stare at the cracked and peeling edges of the polish on my toenails, visible in the eerie glow from the numbers on his digital alarm clock. He stands over me, me who's still crying, who's still naked. He takes a fleece blanket crumpled at the foot of the bed and drapes it over me, then plants a light kiss on my forehead. The tenderness of these actions startles me. Makes me feel worse, makes me cry harder. He sighs again.

"I'll leave you to get dressed," he says. "Then let's get you home."

Dirty. I feel dirty. Dirtier still when he pulls the truck up to my building and doesn't even put the thing in park, just rests his foot on the brake. He doesn't say anything—what could he possibly say?—and I don't either, but I can't seem to get out of the truck.

Finally I say, "I don't even know your name."

"Jasper," he says. "Jasper Douglas."

"You have two first names."

"Something like that." He smiles weakly.

He doesn't ask me my name or my number. I don't ask him to call me. Nothing I've ever seen in movies or heard about from friends has prepared me for this moment. I fumble with the door handle, finally get it to work. "Thanks for the ride," I say, more to my feet than to his face.

"No problem."

I half expect him to squeal away the moment I've slammed the passenger-side door, but he doesn't. In fact, I don't hear him pull away until after I get inside my apartment, door safely locked behind me. It's a gentlemanly thing to do. Benji would approve.

FOUR

I HAD LOVED BATTERY PARK even before Benji took me there, though I let him believe he was the one to introduce me to the quiet splendor of its willow trees and murky creeks, slyly tucked away in a corner of Old New Castle. For Benji, the park, closer to home than the ocean, became a sanctuary—a place to think, a place to play, a place to find himself whenever he felt lost. Which in the months before he left for California was pretty often.

So I guess it's fairly appropriate that this is where I head early the next morning. I pull up to the wharf and park my pumpkin-colored Honda Civic—the Coach, Benji called it because of the color. He had nicknames for everything and everybody, except me. Jack was the Jazzman; Ellie was Impy, as in Imp of Happiness. I was almost always Bridget, occasionally Bridge.

Grasping my beaten-up marbled composition book in one hand, I make my way to the rickety wooden pier that stretches over a section of the river. The muddy water that edges the park flows steadily. I stare at it for a minute, then drop down to the pier's cold planks. From my back pocket, I pull a blue Uniball pen, open the notebook, and begin.

Occasionally I come to the park and write a letter to Benji. I know it sounds cheesy, but it's something I need to do. It's as though if I don't tell Benji when something happens, then it hasn't really happened. If I can't tell him what I'm feeling, then I'm not feeling anything at all.

> *Dear Benji,*
>
> *I'm a mess. I know, I know—what's new? But this is different. This isn't me freaking out because Mr. Hooch gave me a C on my calculus final. It isn't even how I was when Katharine was trying to have my dad arrested.*
>
> *This is you being gone.*
>
> *This is you being everywhere, except where I need you to be.*

Here I pause, chewing the cap of my pen. It sounds so selfish. *Everywhere except where I need you to be.* As if he had a choice.

But he did have a choice, once. No one forced him to go to California. He wanted to go. Desperately.

"New Castle," he'd snort. "This place is a pit, and you know it."

And maybe I did. Other than the park, my only real attachments to Delaware were him and Ellie, and maybe Fitzi. Until it came time for him to choose a college, I thought Benji felt the same no matter what he said.

"Delaware's a good school," I said petulantly.

Benji rolled his eyes. "Yeah, if you're headed for a career at DuPont. Which I'm not. Why are you so hell-bent on my staying, anyway? There's nothing here for me."

"What about me?"

"What about you?"

"Never mind."

So it wasn't really a surprise when Benji applied to the oceanography program at Humboldt State the fall of his senior year. And it wasn't really a surprise when he got accepted. Even his accepting their acceptance didn't throw me for that huge a loop because I knew he would never actually go. I knew that in the end, he wouldn't be able to leave me behind.

But he did leave, and I helped him do it. I made careful lists of things he would need to take with him, then lists of things he could buy once he reached Arcata. I ordered him a museum-produced address book with an iridescent jellyfish on its cover—jellyfish were Benji's main passion—and copied into it the names and numbers of people he might like to keep in touch with. I even helped him pack.

The sun is almost up now, casting crimson shadows on

the opaque water. I fish around my pocket for a crumpled pack of Marlboro Lights, light one, and inhale deeply. Normally I feel too self-conscious to smoke at the park—Benji hated smoking and would feign an obnoxious cough around anyone who tried to light up around him—but not today. Not after last night's debacle with Jasper Douglas. The back of my head buzzes lightly, and I shut my eyes, looking for a sign in the blackness.

I stub my cigarette out on a burnt knob of wood, then place the butt in my pocket. The notebook with the half-written letter rests in my lap. I slam it shut and retreat to the Coach.

As I pull back out onto Route 273, I wonder if I should stop at the Gilberts' house. It's been weeks since I've seen them—I don't think I've even spoken to Anna since her first day at Haley High. I should go, really, but I pass the turn to their house before I can make up my mind. So I just go home instead.

The message light on my answering machine blinks the number three—all messages from Ellie, all left within the space of an hour. She gets progressively frantic with each one, apologizing profusely for abandoning me and assuring me that Marcus flirted with every girl there and was hardly worth it. *Beep!* I erase them all without even thinking about calling her back.

I replay the incidents of the past twenty-four hours in my mind. I cannot stop thinking about them. For one thing, I am not the kind of person who has sex with a stranger. I mean, I didn't lose my virginity until I was seventeen, and that was with *Benji,* who I'd known forever. More disturbing is the fact that I can't stop thinking about him. Jasper. How incredible he smelled, and how incredible I felt when we kissed.

Ellie would understand, if I told her. She's been with a lot of boys. But Ellie would understand on a purely physical level. She wouldn't be able to grasp the full extent of my transgression. The masochistic part of me toys with the idea of confessing to Katharine, but what would I say? "Hey, Mom—guess what? It turns out I really *am* a whore?" No, the only person I could really talk to about this is Dr. Margie, and I'm not scheduled to see her for two whole days.

With a heavy sigh, I head into the bathroom for what will be my third shower in the past twelve hours. But no matter how hot I make the water, or how hard I scrub at my skin, I can't remove the shame of what I've become.

FIVE

FOR THE REST OF THE WEEKEND, I give myself permission to slide into the Hole. The Hole is the place I go to fall completely apart. It's not a fun place—hence the name. But being there is sort of like popping one of those under-the-skin zits on your chin: prickly and painful, but satisfying nonetheless. Eventually all the poison seeps out, you heal, and only a faint scar lingers, a subtle reminder of the war.

Depressions are a lot like snowflakes—no two are exactly alike. Some people get drunk and puke up the badness into a public toilet. Some find a willing stranger and fuck their brains out in the backseat of a rusty Camaro. The Hole requires a lot less energy. In the Hole, time does not exist. Bathing is usually optional. I set the phone's ringer to Off, suit up in sweats, slip under the flannel sheets of my futon, and watch eighties movies on TNT: *Back to the Future,*

Tootsie, Steel Magnolias, The Golden Child. I chain-smoke from the comfort of my bed, even though I hate the lingering smell of smoke in my apartment. There's Easy Cheese on Ritz for breakfast, Cheerios with chocolate milk for dinner.

The Hole is a deceptive place. Even when I've fallen deep within its blackness, I can still talk myself out of bed and into my waitressing uniform. I do my job on automatic pilot, then flee to the safety of home. Ellie gets completely freaked when I slip into Hole mode, but Dr. Margie, my shrink, says that allowing myself to stew in all that ails me is a good thing.

"Your body's telling you something, and you're *responding*," she says, pumping her small fist in a "go get 'em" way.

There are moments, of course, when I can't surrender completely. I'll think about how empty my days are now that I don't have school as a distraction, and I'll wonder if Fitzi was right when he advised me to defer from Del U for a year. Or I'll call Katharine, thinking maybe she has some hidden kindness I've yet to unearth, but these exercises in futility usually end with one of us slamming the phone in the other's ear. Sometimes I'll pick up my neglected sketch pad, blow the quarter inch of dust off its cover, and try to draw the pictures that cloud my head: Benji sleeping. Benji eating spaghetti. Benji playing tackle Frisbee in the park with Anna and his brother, Charlie, and me.

But all my Benjis look the same. Benji dead, in a polished cherry box, eyelids closed, with Frankenstein stitches holding them in place.

———

Monday is Margie day. I roll out of bed promptly at 8:45 and somehow manage to arrive at her office—really just an addition to her suburban Newark home—a full five minutes early for our standing nine o'clock appointment. Dr. Margie is never on time, so I usually sit on the steps, peeved by the delay, and smoke and throw the butts in her seasonal flower garden.

"Bridget," she says through the screen door. She motions me in with her hand. This is part of the routine. Each week, I follow her through the hallway to the wicker-furniture room where she asks me questions and I squirm. It's funny, because Dr. Margie is one of the only people in the world who, at a mere four foot ten, makes me feel tall. I look at her—with her unruly salt-and-pepper hair, with her baggy cream leggings cuffed twice on the bottom, with her teddy-bear-appliqué sweatshirt—and I think, *This is the woman who's in charge of my mental health.*

Dr. Margie slides into her hand-carved rocking chair, clutching a giant mug close to her chest. "Sooo," she says, dunking a peppermint tea bag over and over and over. "How have you been?" She punctuates this question with a bright smile, as if we are two friends having breakfast instead of doctor and patient.

"Okay," I say.

"Mmm-hmm." Dr. Margie begins her weekly inspection, dark marble eyes taking in my unwashed hair, my makeup-free skin, my wrinkled long-sleeved T-shirt with a smudged blob of yesterday's Easy Cheese dotting the belly-button region.

"I had a date," I lie, lifting my chin.

"Mmm-hmm. And how was that?"

Nothing fazes that woman. "Well, it wasn't really a date."

"How do you mean?"

I take a minute to try to arrange the words into an explanation that won't make me feel like throwing up, but I don't quite get there. "I went to a party," I mumble. "I met a boy."

"Oh?" Dr. Margie seems intrigued. "Do you want to tell me about him?"

"Not really."

"Oh."

It's easier than popping a balloon, how quickly she deflates, and I'm filled with a perverse sense of pride. Dr. Margie takes a small, tentative sip of tea, then sets the mug down. "Well, Bridget, I've been thinking. I'd like to talk to you about your dad today."

I freeze. "What?"

"Your father. We haven't talked about him yet and I think it would be helpful, for both of us, if we did."

"What does my father have to do with anything?"

"Good question," Dr. Margie says. "That's what I'm hoping to find out."

"I'm not here to talk about my dad."

"I know," she says, granting me a patient smile. "But

sometimes losing a parent to a long absence can feel like a death."

"What about my mother?"

"Would you rather talk about your mother?"

"No."

"Well."

I look at her, rocking gently in her chair. "So what do you want to know?"

She picks a legal-size notepad off the doily-covered end table and rests it gently in her lap. "Let's start from the beginning. Your parents divorced when you were three, right? But you continued to see your dad on a regular basis."

I nod. "On the weekends, until I turned fourteen. That's when he left."

"And you haven't seen him since?"

"No. I get a birthday card every now and then. Usually with some cash stuffed in the envelope. But no return address or anything. Different postmark every time."

Though her eyes are locked on mine, Dr. Margie scribbles furiously on the legal pad. "So you've had no real contact with him in the last five years."

"Right."

"Do you know why he left?"

"Yes."

She leans forward a bit. "Why?"

"Because Katharine tried to have him arrested. Because he stopped paying child support."

"I see." Dr. Margie's lips purse slightly, but only for a second. Her face goes blank, like an Etch A Sketch after it's been shaken half a dozen times. Then she says the thing she always says, the thing that makes me want to shove that legal pad down her antagonizing throat: "And how did that make you *feel*?"

"How do you think I felt?" I let my fingernails dig deep into the armrests of my wicker chair. "How would you feel?"

"You seem angry," she says mildly.

"Sorry."

"No need to apologize. You're feeling your feelings. That's good." She taps her pen lightly on her knee. "What do you think you'd say to your dad if he were here right now?"

"I don't know."

Silence.

"Let's try something new." Dr. Margie smiles brightly. She pops up from the rocking chair, disappears into the adjoining kitchen, and returns with a wicker chair identical to the one I am sitting on. "This," she says, placing it in front of me, "is your father."

I look at the pink carnations blooming on the cranberry-colored cushion, then up at Dr. Margie's relentlessly pleasant face. "This is my father," I echo.

"Pretend," she says, sinking back into her rocking throne. "Pretend this is your father. Talk to him. Tell him what you're feeling this very moment."

"What I'm feeling," I say, "is that I'm not really into talking to a wicker chair."

"Mmm-hmm." She scribbles something in the margin of the pad. "Bridget—why do you come here each week?"

I was beginning to wonder the same thing. "I don't know."

"What do you hope to accomplish?"

"Accomplish?"

"What are you getting out of these sessions?"

I sigh. "Not a whole lot, apparently."

Dr. Margie carefully places her notepad on the end table and scoots the rocker a bit closer to me. "I think I can help you work through some of this," she says. "But I need your help."

"So I help you by talking to a chair?"

"Forget the chair," she says. "This isn't about the chair. This is about you. This is about what you're willing to bring to this room. It's not enough to show up once a week and think that's going to make a difference. That's like someone thinking they're going to get in shape just by standing in the lobby of a gym. Therapy's like exercise, Bridget. You have to want results. You have to work hard to get those results. It isn't easy, it isn't fun, but in the end, most people feel a hell of a lot better."

I think about this speech as I leave the office. What are we paying this woman for, anyway? I rarely feel better after these sessions, fifty-minute exercises in self-restraint. Two dollars a minute—annoying even if it is Fitzi who's footing the bill.

The wind whips cold at my cheeks. I turn from Chapel Street onto Main and see a couple chatting on the corner. The girl, who couldn't be much more than a freshman, is propped up on a brick storefront, digging her hands into the pockets of her down jacket. Her boyfriend is grinning, leaning into her, tugging on a lock of her dark hair. The girl pulls her hands out of her pockets long enough to teasingly push him away, then pull him close. Then the boyfriend grabs her around the waist and plants a kiss flat on her mouth. The kiss breaks, he takes her hand, and they walk off. I am so intent on the scene unfolding in front of me, I don't realize I have stopped walking and started staring until there is no longer anyone to stare at.

SIX

DUE TO A WICKED ELECTRICAL STORM the following week, I lose cable—my main mode of escape. So I pull on my raincoat and a pair of red vinyl boots and head out to the trusty Blockbuster over in College Square. The rain is so bad that even though I drive to the shopping center, the walk from my car to the store leaves me drenched. I step through the glass door and am assaulted by a blast of air-conditioning so cold it makes my bones ache.

And then I see him. Standing about three feet away, on the right-hand side of the New Releases wall, shelving a whole basket of movies. Embarrassment warms my chilled skin from foot to scalp. A magnetic force pulls me toward him until I'm only inches away.

"Hi," I say.

I expect a flash of recognition to cross his face, but he

43

barely even blinks more than once, just smiles enough for a single dimple to appear.

"Hey." He puts the basket down on the carpet. "Can I help you find something?"

"No," I say, a little too quickly. "I mean, I don't know what I want."

"Of course," he replies. "I should have known."

I get the feeling his comment is meant to be at least somewhat snarky, but it's delivered with such charm that if there is a passive-aggressive undercurrent, it's barely perceptible.

"So," he says.

"So."

Jasper pretends to lean against the wall of videos, tipping an imaginary cap. "Come here often?"

I smile weakly. "Sometimes."

He straightens up. "And your boyfriend? Does he come here, too?"

No mistaking the intention of that comment. "I don't have a boyfriend anymore." My throat closes tightly. Then my eyes start to itch, a precursor to crying, like lightning before a storm. I turn on my heel and head for the door, make it onto the sidewalk before I hear Jasper yelling from behind.

"I'm sorry," he says, jogging toward me. "I'm not usually such a dick. Really." I stop, let him catch up. "I'd never done that before, you know. Taken someone home like that. It kind of freaked me out."

"Shut up, okay? Just shut up."

"Don't cry," he says, touching my arm. "I don't want to be the guy who always makes you cry."

I start bawling then, so much that I don't even mind when Jasper puts his arms around me, cups the back of my head with his hands. "Shhh," he says soothingly. "It's okay. It's going to be okay."

When my sobs subside, he says, "C'mon. Let's get you something to drink." He takes my hand and leads me across the parking lot, over to the grocery store. Inside, he grabs a travel pack of Kleenex and a bottle of chocolate milk, which he pays for.

"Why are you doing this?" I ask.

"Doing what?"

"Being so nice to me."

"I don't know," he says. "You look like you could use some 'nice.' "

We walk back to my car. I try to thank him, but he shrugs me off. Then he takes a pen from his smock pocket and writes his phone number on the side of my hand. "If you ever want to talk, just give me a ring."

"Okay," I say.

I call him the very next day.

Our conversations are awkward at first, but I guess that's to be expected. We begin by covering safe topics like where we grew up, what kind of music we listen to, what our favorite kind of food is.

Me: New Castle, Delaware; chick rock and Brit-pop; extra-meaty lasagna.

Jasper: Garfield, New Jersey; blues and jazz; chicken-fried steak and eggs.

Jasper tells me he's a black man trapped in the body of a white boy. I tell him I'm a forty-year-old trapped in the body of a would-be coed. He asks me why I postponed college; I say breezily that I needed time to find myself. I actually stole that line from my aunt Dorrie, who was third in her premed class and dropped out her senior year for a part-time job in a pizza parlor. Jasper, it turns out, is a biochem major and is eyeing a career at DuPont.

Every time we talk I vow to myself that I will explain what happened the night of our first encounter, and every time I completely lose my nerve. A couple of random calls morph into a nightly marathon session, and the more intimate our talks become, the less capable I feel of confessing my past. Jasper's been so great, and when I talk to him, I don't have to be Bridget the Mourner. He knows there was once a Benji and now there is not, but he just assumes we broke up, and I haven't cleared the misconception. It's easier this way, I think.

Two weeks pass before Jasper first pops the question. Dinner and a movie, nothing too terribly scary. Only it is petrifying, not just because it would be my first post-Benji date, but because I'm growing to rely on Jasper's midnight phone calls. I actually look forward to them. There was one night that I had to work until two A.M., and Jasper had a test the following day, so we didn't get to talk. It shouldn't have been a big deal, but it was. My whole body felt itchy and uncomfortable. The itch didn't stop until he called the next day.

So I decline, as warmly and politely as possible. "It's not you," I tell him. "It wouldn't be fair—I don't want to date anyone right now."

"So don't call it a date," he replies. "Call it two people mutually participating in a random activity."

This makes me smile despite myself. So, after four more attempts on Jasper's part, I cave:

"What would you do if I said yes?"

"I'll pick you up tomorrow at eight," he says smoothly. "Talk to you then."

He hangs up before I know what hit me.

SEVEN

JASPER ARRIVES AT EXACTLY 7:56 P.M. I know this only because I've been ready for a full half hour and have passed
the extra time watching the numbers change on the VCR
clock. I haven't seen him since the night at the Blockbuster
nearly three weeks ago, and I've forgotten how attractive he
really is, with those tousled brown curls pouring over his
eyes. He's wearing a fifties-style black bowling shirt with the
name Buzz sewn on the front in a loopy orange stitch. His
tan chinos bear fresh creases, and I notice that his steel-toed
Doc Martens have been buffed to a high shine.

"I brought you something," he says with a grin, handing
me a bunch of sunflowers wrapped in green floral paper.

"Thanks," I say, swallowing hard. I step through the door-
way, clutching the sunflowers in one hand.

"Shouldn't you put those in some water?"

48

"Right," I say. "Water."

When I return, Jasper offers me his arm. It's a strong arm, lean, with taut muscles. And so tan, even now, in the middle of October. As he unlocks the passenger-side door of the truck, I stare at my saddle shoes and try to banish thoughts of tan muscles from my mind.

"Great shoes," Jasper says before shutting the door.

Who is this guy? I think, steeling my eyes to a windshield smudge.

"Don't you wanna know where we're going?" he asks, pulling onto I-95.

"Sure," I say.

"Ever hear of a place called Fat Rick's?"

I shake my head.

"So it'll be a surprise then." He flashes me another grin.

I stay silent for most of the twenty-five-minute drive, testing my seat belt every couple of miles. Jasper keeps sneaking peeks at me out of the corner of his eye, and I pretend not to notice.

"You okay?" he asks. "You're awfully quiet."

"What?"

"Nothing."

"It's the highway," I say. "I hate driving on highways."

Jasper pulls into a suburban strip mall in North Wilmington. There, tucked between a camera shop and a take-out Chinese restaurant, stands Fat Rick's Bar-B-Q Blues Bar. Jasper strolls through the parking lot with his hands crammed deep into his pockets, pulling them out only to open the door for me. An enormous black man sits behind the cash register, which is smack in front of us. "Two?"

Jasper nods. "That's Fat Rick," he whispers as we follow the man to our booth. Jasper's palm rests lightly on the small of my back, sending a shiver of unwelcome pleasure down my spine.

"You ever been here before?" asks Fat Rick, slapping down two cardboard menus with a doughy hand.

"She's new," Jasper says, leaning back.

"Oh, you in for a treat tonight, pretty lady." Fat Rick winks at me, then playfully pinches my upper arm. "Tonight we got some of the steamiest zydeco this side of the Mississippi."

"Sounds great," I say. "Can we get it as an appetizer, or does it only come as an entrée?"

Fat Rick howls with laughter, smacking his Jell-O belly for emphasis. "Honey, you don't *eat* zydeco. You dance to it." He turns to Jasper. "You watch out for this one. Lordy, she's *priceless*." He swaggers off to the kitchen, the residue of his laughter increasing the number of knots in my stomach.

"Why don't you order for both of us?" I say, pushing my menu toward Jasper. He nods, and as he surveys the menu, I pretend to be engrossed in a folk-art portrait of some pianist that graces the wall next to our table.

I am infinitely relieved that Fat Rick is not our server this evening. In his place is Sylvie, a much less intimidating figure with shell-capped dreads. Jasper rattles off a list of

items: fried gator strips, hush puppies, pulled pork sand-
wiches with okra relish.

Sylvie returns with two frosted ginger jars of icy lemon-
ade. Jasper rips one end off the wrapper of his straw and
blows it at me. I roll my eyes. A soulful voice pours from
massive speakers situated around the small restaurant.

"Bessie Smith." Jasper raps his knuckles lightly on the
mahogany-colored table. "Man, she's beautiful."

"You like her?"

"Oh, yeah—she's one of the greats. Started out as a
dancer. Kind of a funny story—she was fired from this
vaudeville show celebrating black women because she
wasn't dark enough. Good thing, though—made her turn to
singing."

"How come you know so much about the blues?"

He shrugs. "Always liked it, I guess. Something about the
way it creeps inside you, makes your bones itch."

Our food arrives shortly after. As we munch on the salty-
sweet gator strips, a six-pack of musician types saunters in,
dripping well-worn denim, carved wood necklaces, and
long, floaty scarves fringed with tinkly bells. They silently
begin arranging their gear on a small platform that I guess
serves as a stage. Jasper nods in their direction. "Planet
Folle," he says. "Crazy Planet. They rock."

"You've heard them before?"

"Mmm-hmm," he says, licking some salt off his thumb.
"They always pack the place."

Sylvie brings us heaping plates of food to the sounds of

Planet Folle's lone fiddler tuning up. She shakes her head. "Hear that squawk?" she inquires of no one in particular. "That man's gonna play like the devil."

I pick at my pulled pork sandwich, scooping a few shards of meat with torn-off pieces of the roll.

"Eat," Jasper says. "You look like you haven't in months. And don't give me any of that 'I'm on a diet' crap. Don't you know guys like girls with healthy appetites?"

"Hey, now," I mock growl. "You're not earning any points with that kind of talk."

"Oh, so we're on a point system?"

I heatedly cram an entire hush puppy into my mouth. "There," I mumble, my mouth full. "Better?"

"Hells yeah," he says, grinning yet again.

I self-consciously clean most of my plate, even though the combination of grease and nervousness lies heavy in my stomach. Jasper looks on approvingly as I fight the urge to throw up. The band starts to play.

"C'mon," Jasper says, slipping out of the booth and reaching for my hand. "Let's dance."

"Uh, I don't think so. I'm not feeling so good."

"Please?" he coos. "I'll be your best friend."

"You dance," I offer. "I'll watch."

But Jasper refuses to take no for an answer. He drags me to the front of the stage, where a small group has already begun to form. There's not much of a dance floor, just a small clear spot of hardwood. This does not deter Jasper one bit. He lifts one knee, then the other, shaking his hands and hips to the rhythm blasting from the trumpeter's lips. I stand there motionless.

Jasper leans into me. "How can you be still? I know you know how to move that body." He takes my arms, throws them around his neck. Then he places his hands on my hips and sways them from side to side. "Let it out, Bridget. Let it *all* out."

And I don't know if it's the way his eyes are burning into me, or if I am simply too full of fried food to protest, but I do. Let it out. I match Jasper shake for shake, shimmy for shimmy, let my skirt spin out like cartoon pizza dough. We dance madly until the band takes a break some forty minutes later.

"Need air," I wheeze, pushing sweat-soaked hair off my face. "Be right back."

Outside, I shakily pull a crushed Marlboro from the pocket of my skirt. As I fumble for my lighter, a long-fingered hand holding a match magically appears. It belongs to the trumpeter.

"Thanks."

"Saw you dancing," he says, blowing out the flame. "You and your boyfriend."

I feel my face flush hotter. "He's not my boyfriend."

"That's funny." He takes a long drag off his own hand-rolled cigarette, then lets it drop. "Y'all move like you're lovers."

"Well, we're not."

The man smiles, the corners of his eyes crinkling like

crepe paper. He offers me his hand. "Zeke," he says. "Didn't mean to offend you."

"I'm Bridget," I say, accepting the firm shake. "And no offense taken."

"You staying for the second half?"

"I don't know. Maybe."

He nods as if I've said something really profound. "See you inside." He disappears through the door, leaving me alone in the half-light of the strip-mall sidewalk.

I take a few more puffs of my cigarette, crush it out with a saddle shoe. Then I go back in, making a beeline for our corner booth.

"Can we get out of here?" I ask. "I'm exhausted."

Jasper swallows a mouthful of crushed ice. "Sure. Let me get the check."

I hand him a twenty, then say, "Meet you at the truck."

The cool October breeze feels heavenly on my skin. I let my head rest on the even cooler glass of the passenger-side window. The beginnings of a migraine toy with the tender spot where my head meets my neck.

The drive back to Newark is much like the drive to Wilmington: quiet. Jasper flicks on the radio, settles on the oldies station. I stare out the window, trying to find the moon.

We pull up to my apartment a little after ten. "Thanks," I say. "I had fun." I open the door.

"Wait." Jasper cuts the engine and puts his hand on my

arm. I look at him, waiting for him to speak. He doesn't. I pull the door shut.

"Can I ask you a question?"

"You just did," I reply, unconsciously adopting a Benji-ism.

"Why did you say yes? To me, I mean."

I let my eyes fall to his nose, which seems safer than his eyes. "Why did you keep asking me out?"

"You shouldn't answer a question with a question."

I search my brain, looking for an acceptable response. But the truth eludes me. "I honestly don't know," I say after a long pause.

"Fair enough." Jasper turns the key and revs the engine a bit. "That's all I wanted. You're free now."

"Jasper," I say. Now it is my turn to touch his arm. "This isn't about you."

"What? Is there some other guy?"

I suck some air in through my teeth, let my hand drop onto the black leather seat. "Sort of."

"Your ex-boyfriend," he says. A statement rather than a question. I nod. He sighs.

"Don't," I say, swallowing hard. "I told you I wasn't looking to date anybody. I told you I wanted to be your friend."

"And that Benji guy—how friendly do you get with him?"

"It's not what you think. It's . . . complicated."

"Complicated," he repeats in a flat tone.

I bite my lip, trying not to cry. Part of me wants to tell him everything, to spill out all my secrets. But another part of me wants to slip quietly away. Instead, I say, "I really like you, Jasper."

He lifts his smooth finger up to my cheek. The light touch sends little electric shocks down the length of my spine. I look at him looking at me, trying to see myself through his eyes. But all I see is his sad, sweet face, and before I know it, I am pulling him closer. I close my eyes and let my mouth meet his in a pleasant tangle of lips and tongues and teeth. And for a minute it seems as if everything will be okay, as if this will be enough, for him at least, and maybe even me.

Then he withdraws.

"No," he says.

"No?"

"I don't want it this way."

I nod, open the door, and step out into the shadows. He leans over, palms the twenty-dollar bill back into my hand. Then he pulls the door shut and drives off without even saying goodbye.

EIGHT

THE PHONE RINGS FOUR TIMES before I reach over to pick it up. It's Ellie, managing to sound breezy and breathless at the same time.

"Look," she says, "I'm at work, so I can't talk. But I wanted to let you know Jack Doyle was just in here. He's looking for you."

"Jack? But I thought he was in Boston."

"He was. He came back for homecoming."

Homecoming. Weeks ago Anna asked if I would come over and help her get ready for the dance. I already backed out of helping her pick out a dress—there is no way I can gracefully extricate myself from the predance preparation.

"Bridget? Are you still there?"

"Yeah."

"I gave Jack your new phone number. I hope that's okay."

"Sure," I say. "Fine."

But it isn't fine. I think about the last time I saw Jack, the night of the funeral. We had just finished scattering Benji's ashes off the pier at Battery Park. The ceremony had less of a turnout than the viewing, but all the key players were there—except Action Dan, who was in Europe doing the backpacking thing. Jack, the only one of Benji's friends who'd known him longer than I had, stood apart from our group, and I caught him staring at me more than once. His wet eyes, supported by puffy half-moons only a few shades lighter than eggplant, scanned my face. Searching for something. I suppose he wanted me to look the way he looked— red, raw, sleep-starved. I licked my lips, the gooey gloss coating them catching my tongue, and felt deeply ashamed.

Afterward, Jack came up to me, loosening the bloodred tie knotted tightly at his throat. We just looked at each other for a while, not sure what to say.

Finally, Jack said, "This makes no sense."

I nodded. Jack drew his hand up to the bridge of his nose, pinching back more tears.

"A bunch of us are getting together tonight," he said. "To say goodbye. You'll come, won't you?"

"I don't know, Jack. The Gilberts—"

"Will understand," he interrupted.

"I'll think about it."

Jack grabbed my hands, trapped them between his own. "Please come," he said. "Please."

But I couldn't. I knew what the night would hold—a

marathon of "Remember when?" moments. Stories stained by the sappiness of grief, bigger and better and brighter than reality. Exactly what Benji wouldn't want.

Later Ellie told me they all went to the Denny's on Route 13 (Benji's favorite), ordered Southern Slams (Benji's staple), and stole their coffee mugs (Benji's classic pastime). I was glad I hadn't gone, glad I hadn't stayed at the Gilberts', either. Instead, I had escaped their house not long after sunset, slipping out the door without so much as a goodbye. Back at my mom and Fitzi's place I had crawled into bed, strapped my Walkman to my ears, and listened to Peter Gabriel's "In Your Eyes" over and over again, rewinding the tape so many times the recording got fuzzier and fuzzier until it was eventually eaten by the ancient cassette player. And so I lay there, surrounded by silence. I felt like I did after I drank too much on an empty stomach, a sick queasiness sloshing through my insides, the kind where you know if you could only make yourself throw up you'd feel better.

I'm not sure why the thought of seeing Jack scares me so much. Maybe I'm afraid that if I squint a certain way, he will look, as he often did, like a replicated Benji. Or that he'll speak in Benji-isms, that bizarre collection of made-up words and phrases we all absorbed.

Or maybe I am just afraid that I will look into Jack's eyes and see the same dead thing that lurks within my own.

I spend the rest of the afternoon hiding out in my apartment, screening my calls. The first three are from telemarketers, and I let the machine pick up their auto-delayed pitches. But then, just when I think I'm safe, Anna calls, confirming that I will indeed fulfill my duties as personal stylist before the dance tomorrow. I pick up the phone.

"Do you think you can get here by four? Mom wants you to set my hair, since you're the only one who wraps the ends right. And ooh—what are your thoughts on body glitter? Yea or Nay?"

Like the good faux sister I am, I spend the next fifteen minutes or so discussing the merits of mousse versus gel, and whether or not glue-on lashes are worth the hassle. Finally, wearily, I extricate myself from the call and settle in for a night of John Hughes movies and leftover Chinese.

NINE

THE GILBERTS LIVE IN A TWO-STORY TOWN HOME in suburban New Castle, in a neighborhood that once was populated with middle-class families but has slowly gone the way of low-income housing. Their house is filled with avocado rugs, nubby plaid furniture, wood-paneled walls, and a warm, familiar smell that I once found comforting but that now makes me slightly ill.

In the months before the accident, while Benji was away, I used to visit the Gilberts at least once a week, if not more. Mrs. Gilbert loved to cook for me. Real food, like baked macaroni or meatloaf with ketchup dressing. After dinner, Charlie, Benji's eight-year-old brother, always forced me to go "make nice" with his pet hamster, Wade. Charlie's a nut—he giggles uncontrollably at just about everything I say. He and Anna were always vying for my attention, but

Anna, older and more persistent, usually won. She'd drag me up the stairs to her bedroom and lock the door behind us, and we'd settle in for some good old-fashioned girl talk. She'd tell me about which boys she'd been crushing on and which boys had been crushing on her. It was nice. I'm technically an only child, but since I've spent so much time with Anna and Charlie over the years, I've never really felt like one.

Eventually the kids would go off to bed, and Mrs. Gilbert would open a box of Twinkies and a bottle of cheap chardonnay and tell me about how cranky Mr. Gilbert had become since he started working the night shift, about how hard it was to see her babies grow up and not need her as much. And I would nod sympathetically, give the woman hugs, and tell her I understood and I loved her, which I do, I guess. Mrs. Gilbert isn't perfect, but at least she talks to me as if I'm a real person, a feat my own mother still hasn't mastered.

Since the accident, however, I've found myself making excuses not to go over there. I tell them I have to work or spend time with Katharine. Sometimes I ache for the house, ache for its warm smells and threadbare carpeting, but being there, actually being there, spurs a deeper pain. Benji is gone, and the house knows it.

It takes me more than an hour to prep. I skip the jeans and slide into black palazzo pants, which I pair with a lightweight chenille sweater the color of moss. I accessorize. I spritz perfume on my wrists, my neck, and the back of my hair. Then, suitably armored, I get in the Coach and brace myself for what's to come.

I'm not sure how long I have been parked in front of the Gilberts' house when Charlie bounds out the door. He is wearing purple parachute pants that clash violently with his camouflage T-shirt, and this makes me smile.

"You're here! You're here!" he shouts, sticking his head through the window and planting a kiss on my flushed cheek. "Mom's making carrot cake."

We go inside. I say my hellos. Charlie goes to fetch Wade. Nothing has changed.

"You're certainly looking well," Mrs. Gilbert remarks, beaming. "Your skin is positively luminous." Thank God for Max Factor.

Anna, wrapped in a Chinese-print silk robe, summons me to her room. Her dress is, as she has said, "scrumptious." A pale blue satin strapless with a long, straight skirt slit on one side up to the knee. The kind of thing you'd imagine Marilyn Monroe would've worn to her first formal.

"Beautiful," I say. "But definitely no body glitter."

We head back down to the makeshift beauty parlor Mrs. Gilbert has set up in the dining room. The table is covered in cosmetics, curling irons, and an ancient set of hot rollers. I get to work.

As I wrap strands of Anna's hair around warm, foam-covered rollers, she chatters on about Andy Rockwell, her date. "He's so yummy, Bridge—he's got big brown eyes, like a teddy bear. You'd love him." I nod in the right places and ask the right questions: "How did you meet? How did he ask you out?" Et cetera.

The Andy Rockwell spiel takes us through the curlers and on to the makeup—shimmery eggshell eye shadow with a touch of black liquid liner at the base of the lashes, rosewater blush on the apples of her cheeks, and a thin coat of raspberry gloss on her dainty lips. The now-cool curlers are unrolled, leaving big ringlets bouncing on Anna's shoulders. I spritz hair spray on the spirals, gently pull them apart with my fingers, and step back to survey the results.

"Perfect," I say. "You are a goddess in training. Now go get dressed."

Mrs. Gilbert returns from the basement with a load of laundry, which she deposits in the hallway. She asks me to clear a couple of spaces at the table, cuts us each a slice of carrot cake, and sends Charlie outside to play.

"I've missed you," she says, squeezing my hand. "I think about you every day."

"I've been really busy," I lie. "Work. Settling in to the new apartment. You know."

"Anna talks about you all the time. She brags about her big sister to all her friends."

I nod, take a sip of milk.

"And Charlie—well, you're the only one he hugs. Really."

Again I nod, then drain my glass.

"So." Mrs. Gilbert heaves back in her chair, the weight of her body surrounding her like fluffy bedroom pillows. "Tell me—what's new with you?"

"Not much."

"Oh, don't give me that. I went through Ellie's line in the market last week, and according to her, you've been dating some nice young man. Jason, is that his name?"

"Jasper." I correct her through semigritted teeth.

"That's an odd name," Mrs. Gilbert says, eyes fixed on my face. "Is he from around here?"

I shake my head. "New Jersey."

"Northern or southern?"

"We're not really dating," I say, chewing on a fingernail. "We're barely even friends."

"That's not what Ellie says."

"Ellie's wrong."

Mrs. Gilbert sighs, then stands, taking the empty milk glasses into the kitchen to refill them. Charlie bursts through the front door, runs to me, and gives me a quick, tight hug. "Say bye before you leave, okay?" Before I can agree, he's out the door again.

Mrs. Gilbert laughs, opening a fresh carton of milk. "What did I tell you?" she says in her lilting voice. "He loves you. We all do."

"I know," I reply. I feel like a reproached child.

"Do you?" she asks, pouring the creamy liquid. "Because I hope you know, Bridget, that no matter what, we will always be your family." A pause. "Just like Benji will always be our son." I feel the blood begin to drain from my face as she turns and fixes her steel-gray eyes on me.

This is why I stopped coming.

"I'm going to check on Anna," I say, rising. "I think her date's due here any minute."

As if on cue, Anna appears at the top of the staircase. She descends slowly, like a queen at her coronation. Her hair streams behind her like silken sunshine. The ice-blue satin hugs the soft curve of her hips in just the right way. She's a poem in motion, an aria in pearls.

"Well?" she asks, her face flushed less from rose water than exhilaration.

In my head, I hear Benji's voice. "Look at that," he says. "My sister's a babe."

"I have to go," I say. My voice cracks over the words. "I have to go."

I grab my jacket and fly out the door before anyone can stop me. Clumsily, I jam the key into the ignition, turn it over, and squeal out of the parking lot. A dull throb strikes the front of my skull. I want to run away from this house, or maybe from my life, but this only makes me realize that I no longer have any place to run to.

TEN

WHEN I GET HOME, there's a message from Fitzi on the machine asking me to meet him at O'Friel's at seven. "It's been too long, kiddo," he says in his pleasantly gruff voice. "Don't say no, okay?" I'm prepared to do just that when I get the second message, which is from Jack: "Hey, Bridget. It's Jack. Jack Doyle? Um, I got your new number from Ellie Peterson. Sorry it's so loud—I'm calling from a pay phone at Haley and we just lost. Have you seen this year's marching band? Amateurs, man. Anyway, I'm gonna be up in your area later, so I wanted to know if it would be okay for me to stop by. So I guess I will, 'cause you're not there, and I don't have a mobile—" The machine must have cut him off. I look at my watch; the game must've ended at least three hours ago. I quickly dial Fitzi's cell and tell him I'll see him at the bar.

When my mother met Gerald Fitzsimmons, she was thirty-seven and he eighteen years her senior. They met through Mimi Dwyer, the wife of one of Fitzi's fellow fat-cat DuPonters, a few months after my father had taken off for parts unknown. Mimi's unchallenged matchmaking skills were the main reason Katharine had formed a friendship with her. The alliance paid off.

"You'll love this one, Kath," I heard Mimi tell her before their first date. "He's loaded, of course, and looks like a cross between Robert Wagner and Frank Sinatra. *Quite* the score, if you can land him."

Katharine could, and did. Within the year, they were married and we relocated to Fitzi's refurbished eighteenth-century stone farmhouse in Hockessin. Theirs had been the kind of champagne-and-caviar wedding that made the society pages of *Delaware Today* magazine. They chased it with a monthlong European honeymoon, during which I lived with the Gilberts.

Though I was resistant to him in the beginning, Fitzi turned out to be a pretty nice guy. Unlike Katharine's previous boyfriends, Fitzi never treated me as if I were a piece of unexpected luggage. He didn't ignore me when I walked into the room, and he made extraordinary efforts to get to know me better. During racing season, he'd take me and Benji to Delaware Park, place bets for us, and let us keep the winnings when there were any. He took me lots of places to which Katharine wasn't invited. "Me and the kid need some time," he'd tell her. That used to crack Benji up.

"Sometimes," Benji would muse, "I think Fitzi married your mom because you were part of the deal."

Fitzi doesn't have kids of his own. He and his first wife, Joyce, had been childhood sweethearts. Joyce couldn't conceive and had zero desire to adopt, so Fitzi, though disappointed, agreed to be childless. He lost Joyce to breast cancer a few years before Katharine and I came into his life. I never understood what attracted him to Katharine until I saw pictures of Joyce in her thirties, looking remarkably like a softer, warmer version of Katharine herself. I've often wondered what Dr. Margie would say about *that*.

Another thing about Fitzi: He likes to fix things. Antique cars, mostly, but other things too. Like people. He's the reason Katharine finally gave in and started taking antidepressants last year. He's also the reason for my weekly visits to Dr. Margie. "No shame in needing help," he told me when he presented the idea. "Think of it this way—if you broke your arm and didn't go to the hospital, your arm would eventually heal, right? But would it heal the right way? Your heart's been fractured, kiddo, and you need help setting it straight."

So now I see Dr. Margie and Katharine takes Zoloft, and these things make Fitzi happy.

I arrive at O'Friel's, Fitzi's favorite Irish pub, a full twenty minutes late. His face lights up when he sees me, and he hops off his stool to give me a big Fitzi hug.

"Hey, kiddo," he says. "Good to see you, good to see you."

We move to a table in the back, near the dartboard. Fitzi

orders us two pints of Murphy's—they'd never dream of carding me here, not while I'm with Fitzi—and a double plate of cheese sticks. "Don't tell your mom, okay?" he says. "She's been trying to get me to lay off the fried stuff."

"Like there's any danger I'd tell her," I say. "C'mon, Fitz— you know I talk to you more than I do her."

He shakes his head. "Damn shame, too. She misses you like hell." He reaches into the inside pocket of his sports coat and pulls out a thin paperback. "She got this for you, asked me to deliver it since you haven't been to the house in a while."

The book is milky white, with the title embossed in gold foil: *Releasing the Spirit: 12 Steps to Letting Go of a Loved One's Loss.* The back cover is filled with quotes: a woman who miscarried in her eighth month, an elderly lady whose husband of fifty years got cancer, a guy whose father died when he was only four. I chuckle softly. Sometimes Katharine means well, but she never quite hits the mark.

"See?" Fitzi prods. "She's always thinking about you."

In addition to tinkering with his 1967 British-racing-green MG, Fitzi likes trying to repair the relationship between Katharine and me. The Zoloft was a start; under its influence, Katharine's bark has a lot less bite. But I often think of the Zoloft as a Band-Aid—it masks the wounds, but wounds don't stop festering immediately after they've been placed under cotton and plastic.

Thankfully, Fitzi changes the subject. "So how are you fixed for money, Bridge?"

"I'm okay."

" 'Cause you know, just say the word and I can slip you a little extra."

"I'm *fine,* Fitzi. Really."

He lifts his hands in defeat. "Okay, okay. Jeez. You'd think *I* was asking *you* for money."

"You do want *something,*" I say, gulping my Murphy's. "So what is it?"

He smiles. "You got me."

"Well?"

"I was wondering about your plans for Thanksgiving. I know you've spent the last few ones with the Gilberts, but I think it would mean a lot to your mom if you were with us this year."

If there were a lie detector strapped to Fitzi's arm, the beep would be deafening. Katharine doesn't give two shits where I spend my holidays and we both know it. But I don't say this. Instead, I say, "I never spent Thanksgiving with Mom. I used to go to Aunt Dorrie's, before she and the kids moved to Chicago."

Fitzi chugs some beer. "Wouldn't it be nice? Have a real old-fashioned turkey day, just the three of us?"

"I don't think 'catered' and 'old-fashioned' are synonymous," I say dryly.

He pats my hand. "Just think about it, okay, hon? Sleep on it awhile."

Our cheese sticks arrive; Fitzi polishes off most of the order while we shoot the shit. Mostly he talks about Katharine and her latest passion: horticulture. "We're thinking of getting a greenhouse installed out back."

I roll my eyes. Katharine's "passions" never last longer than a couple of months.

I look at my watch; I'm scheduled to be at the truck stop in a little over an hour. "I have to get going," I say. "I'm on at ten."

Fitzi picks up the check and walks me to my car. He kisses my cheek and tells me to take care, then lifts my chin in his hand. "You're a good kid, you know that? I don't think you hear that enough."

His tenderness catches me off guard, and I guess this registers on my face. "What?" he asks softly. "What is it, Bridge?"

"I don't know," I say, sniffling. "I guess sometimes I forget how lucky I am to have you for family."

ELEVEN

IT'S JUST AFTER TWO A.M., and the Iron Skillet is nearly filled to capacity. The room is divided between the restaurant's two main types of late-night Saturday clientele: rough truckers loading up on caffeine and conversation before heading back to the interstate, and semi-drunk university students taking advantage of the diner's after-hours breakfast buffet.

Most waitresses prefer to have the former in their station—the truckers are often lonely and tend to leave large tips in exchange for some warm conversation, while the students usually get the buffet (puny tips) or are too drunk to calculate fifteen percent of their bills. But I like serving the students better. Their self-possession doesn't allow them to think of me as anything more than a food-bringing machine, which in turn allows me to discard the syrupy waitress façade and simply do my job.

And I like the work, mostly. The polyester of my dirt-brown uniform scratches at my neck and the stress of standing for eight hours at a time swells my feet, but the money's good and the other waitresses are polite enough and, God, at least I'm out of the house.

Tonight, however, a handful of stoned sorority types at table five keep chastising me for not refilling their Diet Cokes fast enough. Then the blondest one yells for me from across the room—"Hey, you. Waitress girl. Could you come here *right now*?"—to order some club soda for the ketchup stain setting into her cream-colored cardigan.

"Um, I don't think we have that here," I say.

"Well, could you at least check? This sweater's *Calvin Klein*."

I do as I am told, only to discover that I was right. When I dutifully report this to the girl, she not only refuses to believe me but also seems offended when I suggest she try the late-night liquor store down the street.

"I want to speak to your manager," she spits out. "You're very *rude*."

Something inside me snaps, and I slam my hand down hard on the chipped tabletop. "Listen, Miss Phi Beta Stupid. We. Don't. Have. Club. Soda. You got that?" As I turn and walk away, I see a couple of truckers two tables over let out big belly laughs. I lift my head, filled with a weird pride over the outburst. Then I see him. Jasper. I blink a few times, surprised at this appearance, and head over.

"Hey," I say, wiping my now-sweaty palms on my apron.

"That was inspired."

"Um, thanks." I feel the weight of his eyes, try to avoid it by looking at the silver buttons on his shirt. "What brings you here?"

"Oh, I don't know," he says. "Had a hankering for some food served on a skillet, I guess."

"That so?"

He tries to keep a straight face, but it soon dissolves into a grin. "I thought you might be here," he says, reaching out and brushing his hand across my sleeve. "When do you get off?"

It takes me less than a minute to find someone willing to cover my tables for the duration of my shift. Then I punch my time card and check out a good hour and a half early.

Back to my apartment. I ask Jasper to wait in the truck while I run upstairs and change. The light on my answering machine is blinking like crazy, but I ignore it. I slip into my nicest pair of date jeans and a soft chocolate suede button-down. After dabbing some almond-scented oil on my wrists, I practically cartwheel back out the door, a big doofus grin on my face.

We head to the Brew Ha Ha on Main Street, but the din of the artsy crowd's philosophizing makes me uncomfortable, so we get Chai tea lattes to go and head right back out again. In Jasper's truck, the radio plays too many songs that remind me of Benji, so I shut it off and tell Jasper to take a right.

We end up at the legendary Kells Point, only a short walk from the university. Its location makes it a favorite among carless students, the bulk of whom tend to be freshmen. Mostly *horny* freshmen, looking for a little privacy from roommates and R.A.s.

I cannot believe I've brought him here.

"Feel like walking?" I ask, touching his arm.

"Yeah. Let's."

The heat of the cup keeps my hands from freezing, but it's the sound of Jasper's voice that's keeping the rest of me warm.

"So I'm glad you came by," I say. "I wasn't sure if I was going to see you again."

Jasper smiles. "Nothing's ever that easy."

We walk. I finish my Chai, discard the empty cup in a nearby trash can. Jasper stops and points to the moon, visible through a veil of mist.

"Look," he says. "How beautiful is that?"

"You know what they're saying about the moon, don't you?" I ask. "They're planning to start colonizing it within the next decade."

"Which 'they' is that?"

"I'm not sure. NASA, I guess. It's been on the news."

Jasper's eyes drop back down to my face. "How do you feel about that?"

"I don't know," I say, looking upward, avoiding his gaze. "I guess I'm in awe. I mean, *ten* years. That's nothing. That's no time at all."

"Does that scare you?"

"Yeah, a little," I say, meeting his eyes now. "It's like the stuff of cartoons, you know? But it's not. It's real and it's going to happen. And it just makes me realize how limitless the world—the universe—really is. And how small and insignificant a part of it I am."

Jasper's mouth catches mine by surprise.

"What was that for?"

"For significance," he says, grinning. "So, tell me more."

"More of what?"

"I don't know. Anything. Just keep talking."

"Okaaayyy." I think for a second. "You know that girl at the Skillet? The one I was yelling at? Well, for a long time, I totally avoided people like that. I thought they were just disgustingly self-absorbed. But now I wonder."

"Wonder what?"

"Maybe I was the one who was so self-absorbed. You know? I mean, they say you criticize in other people the thing that you hate most about yourself, right?" I feel my cheeks heat with embarrassment. The thoughts that seemed so smart in my head sound silly in my ears. Am I destined to ruin this thing before it even starts?

A small smile teases the corners of Jasper's lips. "You're big into this concept of an almighty 'they,' aren't you?"

"I guess I never really thought about it."

"Don't look so sad," he says, tugging on the sleeve of my jacket. "It was just an observation."

"I'm not sad," I say.

"You're not happy."

"I'm happy you came tonight."

And there's the grin. There is something in that grin that makes me feel safe, as if I've come home. And maybe this is what scares me most.

The grin morphs into a head cock. He asks, "So what else makes you happy?"

"I don't know," I say. "I think I'm more in tune to what *doesn't* make me happy."

"What about sliding? Does sliding make you happy?"

"Excuse me?"

"Sliding." Jasper points to the shiny double-width children's slide that fits two adults comfortably. "That thing's begging to be used." I am grateful for his ability to rescue a potentially dangerous conversation at the moment before implosion. I let my shoulder gently bump his as we cross the park.

The cold of the metal slide sends a tiny jolt through my body, or maybe it's the feel of Jasper's hand resting on my knee.

"You ready?"

"You know," I say, cocking my own head, "I think maybe I am."

We drive to my house. Jasper puts the truck into park but doesn't cut the engine. A pebble of anxiety embeds itself in my chest. I realize that I don't want him to leave yet, but I'm also not ready to invite him in. So I simply thank him for the evening, kiss his cheek, and say good night.

Later, long after he's gone, I sprawl out on my futon, watching *Viva Las Vegas* on the Spanish channel. I think of Jasper's kisses at the park, how they were hot and sweet and truly comforting. I think of how he pressed my face closer to his, one hand behind my head, the other on my cheek, as if he was afraid I'd run away.

But then I look up, and I see Benji's portrait watching me from its post in the shrine, and the sweetness gives way to sadness and anger and regret. I quickly shed my clothes and slip into bed.

TWELVE

IT IS SPRING. *The air sweats a balm of daffodils and honeysuckle and rain. We are driving back from seder at my aunt Dorrie's house, stuffed with gefilte fish and brisket and matzo ball soup. An all-brass arrangement of the Little Fugue in G Minor blasts from the Coach's tinny speakers, surrounding us in a pleasant cacophony of tuba and trumpet and slide trombone.*

When it has finished, Benji sighs heavily, blissfully. As he pushes Rewind, he says, "You know how when you're listening to a really powerful piece of music like that, you can feel it, in your chest and stuff? And it's like some invisible hand just reaches into you and squeezes something, not your heart or anything clichéd like that, but something, *and if it pushes it one way, you'll burst into tears, and if it pushes it another, you'll crack the widest smile, and if it pushes it another, you'll just curl up into a little ball and fall fast asleep." Pause. "I'm beginning to think that's what love must feel like."*

His words come out in a flurry, but once they are spoken we both know what will follow.

"And me?" I ask, eyes darting from car to car on the road ahead. "Do you get that chest feeling when you think of me?"

Silence. His sharp breath. More silence. My own soft sigh.

Automatically, I drive to the park, but not to the wharf. Instead, I pull the car into a side street that overlooks the water and stare at the yellow reflection of the waning moon.

"I can't do this anymore," I say.

Benji says nothing. I do the same.

Finally: "You know I love you."

"Yes," he says. "I know."

In the religion of love, Benji was an agnostic. He signed his letters "See ya" or "Later" or only with his name. He said that "I love you" was a sentence tossed around thoughtlessly and that in the process it had lost all semblance of meaning. He said romantic love was a concept invented by poets looking to get laid and perpetuated by movie studios, pop musicians, and greeting-card companies wanting to boost sales. He said sex was an expression of a physiological drive to procreate, and love was the lie people told each other in hopes of securing a long-term partner in that pursuit.

I suppose Benji's attitudes toward love and sex make sense if you think about the house he grew up in. I know my own views on these subjects have been colored by the actions of my parental units. But I always held the hope that love *is* real, it *does* exist, that I'd found it in Benji, and that one day, he'd realize he'd found it in me, too.

I think back to the night before he left for California—the night of our first and only time together—and how he told me that he did love me, and that I had been the one to teach him what love was. But then I remember the letter that arrived a week before he flew home that last Christmas. The one I have never told anyone about, not even Ellie.

> *I don't think love can be reduced to an equation. Friendship + Attraction ≠ Love. I wish we could go back to being just friends but I'm not sure that's possible. Please don't call me or write me or try to change my mind. It will only make things hurt more.*

And so I'm left wondering this: Which was more real? The tender postcoital declaration or the carefully scripted dispatch, the one he professed to have written and re-written on three separate occasions?

And then there's this: Does it even matter now?

Jasper and I have agreed to take it slow, whatever that means. I think in our case, *slow* refers to how long we delay having sex again, since we've been seeing each other regularly. Emotionally, we're already fairly naked. A typical conversation will go something like this:

JASPER: I passed a limo on the way to pick you up.

ME: Oh, yeah?

JASPER: They kind of freak me out.

ME: Why's that?

JASPER: I always think the people inside are so important. Like they're big and powerful and deserving of such a long car. But the few times I've actually ridden in one I felt like a dork. It's totally a metaphor for my life. Like, all the fabulous things I've done aren't really that cool. Everyone else's lives are so much better.

When he says things like this, I need to touch him, even if it's just my hand on his knee. It's as if I'm trying to make sure he's an actual person and not some imaginary being I dreamed up out of loneliness.

And then there are other times, other questions I'm not ready to answer. He'll ask me why we don't ever go to my apartment, even when we just pick up a pizza and a movie. What can I say? Because the walls are covered with pictures of my dead boyfriend? Once he actually said, "I get the feeling that even when you're with me, you're not really with me," and I couldn't argue with him, because the truth is, half the time I'm haunted by the thought that this is wrong, that it's too soon, that falling in love with someone else will obliterate the love I felt before.

I've been avoiding Ellie lately, though I'm not sure why. Maybe it's because every time we talk she asks me about

Jasper. She deconstructs our relationship with a precision Dr. Margie would rightfully envy. Somehow her questions feel too obtrusive. Or maybe it's that this thing I have with Jasper is too fragile to bear the weight of Ellie's constant analysis.

Today, however, there's no escaping contact. It's Ellie's nineteenth birthday, and we're spending the day in Baltimore, as we have done on each of Ellie's birthdays since she first got her license. We swing by the Skillet for a quick breakfast on our way out of town, and then Ellie hops on I-95 South. I try not to squirm too much, try to have faith in her driving ability, no matter how much highways spook me. The sixty-minute ride is filled with the sound of Ellie's chipper prattle, alternating with good-time oldies played too loud. I say next to nothing, other than conversational fillers such as "yeah" and "uh-huh." We hit traffic at the Harbor Tunnel and crawl at an excruciating pace to our first destination: the National Aquarium.

Now, I like the aquarium. It's a good aquarium. I've been there a thousand times, yet on each visit I discover something new. However, the last time I went was last December, when Benji came home and we took Anna and Charlie to celebrate the beginning of Christmas break.

There's a chapter in the new grief book Katharine sent that talks about how to deal with certain places that trigger intense, often painful memories of a person who's died. The author says it doesn't help to avoid those places; instead, you should visit them with a supportive friend or family member and try to focus on the happy things you and the deceased did or experienced there. She suggests visualizing each painful memory as a dark blue balloon that inflates and turns pink with each happy thought you conjure up. When the memory is "full," she says, you should knot off the balloon and tie a string to the nub. Then, when you have gathered as many pink balloons as possible, you're supposed to let go of the strings—and, ultimately, let go of the ghost that haunts each location.

I am prepared to attempt this exercise, even though just reading about it made me feel like an idiot. But then, as we are paying to get in, I see the huge promotional display for the featured exhibit: JELLIES: PHANTOMS OF THE DEEP.

Without a word to Ellie, I begin heading toward Level Three, where the exhibit is housed. "Hey, wait up!" she calls after me, but I don't slow. I barely even hear her.

I am at the gallery's entrance before I know it. The space is completely dark, save for the eerie purplish glow emanating from the many tanks built into the walls. There are jellyfish *everywhere*. Hundreds of them, gliding, flowing, dancing, shooting through the tanks. I recognize a couple of species from the glossy coffee-table books Benji collected, like the steel-blue moon jelly, which floats like an enormous squashed marshmallow in the gently undulating water. I touch my fingers to the glass, not even realizing that I am doing so until one of the guards politely asks me to remove them.

Over the creepy New Age music being piped into the

room, I hear Ellie's breathy voice: "Jesus, Bridget. Have you ever *seen* anything so beautiful?" Together, we walk the perimeter of the small room, marveling at the delicate creatures. And then we see the so-called elegant jellies. Benji's favorites. Each one less than an inch long, round and clear, like a fluorescent dream catcher. Under the tank's lights they twinkle silver, thousands of them moving together like finely choreographed shooting stars.

"You're crying," Ellie says, startled. I reach up and touch my cheek, surprised at the moisture.

"It's nothing," I say. "Allergies."

Thankfully, she doesn't press for more.

We tour the space a second time, slowly and less hungrily, reading the placards by the tanks. Some of the stuff I know from Benji's incessant rambling, like that jellyfish don't have hearts, brains, bones, or eyes. "I like my women like I like my jellies," he'd quip. "Headless and heartless."

Ellie grows bored long before I do and is eager to visit the permanent rain forest exhibit on Level Two. I tell her to go on ahead and I'll catch up in a few. I'd rather she not be here anyway. But it's as if she knows that's what I'm craving, and disapproves, and so she doesn't grant me even a second to myself.

"This is starting to feel weird," she says. "Let's move on, okay?"

But I can't move on. I'm frozen, my feet planted firmly in front of the elegants, my eyes transfixed by their tiny transparent bodies.

A DEAD JELLYFISH CAN STILL STING, AS LONG AS ITS TENTACLES REMAIN WET.

My legs feel weak; my throat dry. The small, dark room suddenly suffocates me. I have to get out, I have to escape. "I need a drink," I tell Ellie, and we head to the snack bar.

I don't talk much through the rest of our aquarium tour. Ellie too is strangely quiet. After forty-five minutes of silent strolling, she turns to me and says, "Do you want to skip the Hard Rock and just head home?"

"It's your birthday."

"Yeah," she says. "I know."

And so we leave. I stare out the window as Ellie does eighty on the back roads of Maryland, up north to the Delaware border. We reach my apartment in record time. I notice for the first time that Ellie's jaw is tight and her eyes slightly red. "I'm sorry," I say. "I didn't mean to spoil your day."

She shrugs. "Whatever."

I reach into the backseat and pull out the Hello Kitty gift bag of birthday presents I stashed back there when she first picked me up. "Here," I say. "These are for you."

"Thanks."

"Do you want to open them?"

"Maybe later."

"Oh."

Ellie revs the engine. She seems impatient to be free of me.

"I told you I'm sorry," I mumble. "I don't know what else I can say."

"Maybe you shouldn't be *saying* anything," she snaps. "Maybe it's something you should be *doing*."

I don't know how to respond to that.

She sighs heavily. "When you told me about Jasper, I thought maybe you were getting somewhere. Getting away from the past. But you're not, Bridge. You're stuck in your memories. You're like the kid who tries to run down the up escalator at the mall. It's killing you. And it's killing everything you touch."

I climb out of the car and she pulls away without saying goodbye. I trudge up the steps to my apartment, the weight of her words bowing my back.

THIRTEEN

WHEN WE WERE IN HIGH SCHOOL, Jack Doyle toted around his trumpet the way folksingers lug their acoustic guitars. He played constantly, regardless of venue (school cafeteria, pool party, Battery Park), and through the years, the pads of his fingers grew thick as pink gummy erasers. He prided himself on that dead skin, which he explained was the mark of a seasoned musician. The trick, he said, was to play through the pain. Calluses don't come easy. First there are the blisters, popping and peeling and forming crusty yellow scabs. Then more blisters, more scabs, until finally, one day, they don't come back. Numbness sets in. Then, and only then, can you play pain free.

So with this principle in mind, I slip *Little Earthquakes* into my CD player and program it to spin track seven, "China," an infinite number of times. I crank the volume and cross to the futon, where I lie flat on my back. At first I feel ridiculous, as if I'm the star of some teen soap opera on the WB. But then Tori Amos's voice touches me like a bad sunburn, stinging my skin with hot prickles, the lyrics lacerating all logic, unleashing tears so fierce I feel as if my eyeballs will pop out of my head. The pain seeps into my body, hot water on a block of ice, cracking, splitting, melting me down into a shifting, shapeless puddle of hurt. I clutch my stomach, sore from the sobs.

God, I miss him.

My mind spews memories like a movie montage: Benji twisting sheets of leftover tin foil into a troupe of wacky disco dancers at the lunch table. Benji riding shotgun in the Coach, sticking his head out the window like a puppy, howling into the nothingness as I break eighty on the back roads of Hockessin. Benji lying next to me under my favorite willow tree in the park, both of us watching the squirrels that chase each other around its twisted trunk, making up stories about the Big Things we'll do once our Real Lives begin.

> *Sometimes, I think you want me to touch you.*
> *But how can I, when you build the Great Wall around you.*
> *In your eyes, I saw a future together.*
> *But you just looked away, into the distance. . . .*

And this goes on for at least an hour, maybe more. Eventually, Jack's trick works, and I do become desensitized to the song, and then I realize that I'm finally ready to do the thing Ellie's been wanting me to do since Benji died some nine months ago. Only I'm not doing it for her—I'm doing it for us. For me and Jasper. Because I know now there can't really be a me and Jasper—a me and anybody—if there's still a me and Benji.

It's time to dismantle the shrine.

One by one, I lift the frames from the hooks I hammered into the wall and wrap them in soft folds of acid-free tissue paper, taking great care not to look at the pictures trapped beneath the glass. I place each one gently in a big sweater box. I lay the last one, Benji's senior portrait, on top of the stack, seal the box with several layers of duct tape, and carry it down into the basement, where I tuck it behind the red plastic bin of stuffed animals Katharine made me take when I moved out.

On to Phase Two. I call Ellie's cell phone. She answers on the fifth ring.

"Where are you?" I ask.

"At home," she says.

"Can I come over?"

"Are you still mopey?"

"Say yes, okay?"

She does, and I head over, too intent on my mission to light a single cigarette. Ellie opens the door on the second knock. She eyes the stuffed plastic grocery bag I'm grasping in my hands. "What's that?" she asks.

I hand it to her and say, "I need your help."

We gather the necessary supplies and go into the backyard. Ellie fills the inside of a galvanized trash barrel with some newspaper from the recycling pile, douses it with lighter fluid, and hands me a box of kitchen matches. Solemnly I light one and drop it on the soggy pile. A bright orange flame whooshes up loudly, followed by a series of satisfying pops and crackles.

And thus begins the Ceremonial Burning of the Sweatpants. I drop each of the four pairs I've accumulated these past months into the fire. Ellie stays on standby with a mini–fire extinguisher. Once the fabric is charred beyond recognition, she squirts white foam onto the flames. Then she says, "I'm proud of you," and I say, "I'm proud of me too."

FOURTEEN

AFTER I LEAVE ELLIE'S, two things occur. One, I make a conscious decision to skip the back roads and take I-95 all the way to Newark. Two, I skip my apartment and head straight to Jasper's dorm.

I squeal into the visitors' lot and rush to the front of Dickinson A, where a preppy blonde holds the door open for me. I pass her without so much as an acknowledgment. Thank God I don't have to buzz him—I'm scared enough I'm going to lose my nerve.

I take the stairs to the second floor two at a time. The door to Jasper's room must be open; I hear him talking to someone as I head down the hall. When I reach his room, I peep inside. There's a girl sitting on his bed, a redhead, no less. Bitterness replaces excitement as I rap my knuckles against the wood.

Jasper looks up, startled. "Hey, you," he says, grinning. "What are you doing here?"

"Do you have a sec?" I look at the red-haired girl. She doesn't move.

"Sure," he says. "Mel and I were just finishing up."

This Mel person doesn't look pleased, but she loads her notebook into a green velvet bag flung on the floor. "So I'll see you later, Jay?" she asks. I bite the corner of my bottom lip between my teeth. *His name is* Jasper, *you skank-dogger. Now get the hell out of here before I kick your bony ass.*

I smile sweetly as Mel brushes by. "Nice meeting you," I say before shutting the door and turning the lock. I swivel in time to see the tail end of Jasper's confused look. "You okay, Bridget?" he asks. "You look a little . . . off."

"Who was that?"

"Melanie? She's my lab partner." A slow smile spreads across Jasper's face. "I don't think I've ever seen you *jealous* before. It's kind of cute."

I look at a patch of tan skin peeking out from the collar of his crisp white shirt. It would be so easy if we never had to talk. I step toward him, my hands reaching for the buttons. I let my mouth graze the hollow at the base of his throat.

"Um, Bridget? What are you doing?"

His tone is light, playful even. It's a go. I lift my head, keeping my eyes fastened on his mouth. Toss my hair slightly, swishing it across one shoulder blade. He reaches up to touch it, an involuntary response, like one of Pavlov's dogs. I finish with the shirt, gently nudge it onto the floor, then bring my hands down to the button fly of his well-worn jeans. A small *mmm* escapes Jasper's lips.

We move to the bed. Jasper lies flat on his back, pulls me on top of him. It's better this way, I think, without the talking. The talking would only mess it up. Then, as if he has read my thoughts, Jasper breaks our kiss, wiggles out from under me. "What are we doing?" he says. "What's going on with you?"

I touch his cheek, guide his face back toward my own. "Don't you want to have sex?" I say, regretting my words the minute they are spoken. I got it wrong, how could I get it wrong?

"What did you say?"

But it's a rhetorical question. Jasper sits up, refastens the buttons I've just undone. I tuck my face into his pillow, wishing I could sink into the soft T-shirt fabric of its case until it swallowed me whole.

He clears his throat. "Sit up," he says. I do not move. "Bridget," he says, "we need to talk." He tugs at the sleeve of my shirt. I still don't move. Finally, he says, "I'm going to get us a couple of sodas from the basement. Then we'll talk, okay?"

Jasper quietly closes the door behind him. I consider fleeing the scene, but realize this will only make things even more complicated than they already are. No, best to do the talking now, when everything's already fairly fucked up.

He returns bearing two cans of generic root beer. I am sitting on the edge of his bed, still fighting the urge to flee. I crack open the can he hands me and take a deep swig. He sits beside me. I mumble an apology. He doesn't respond.

I take a deep breath. "Why are you so afraid to touch me?"

"Why are you so afraid I won't?"

"I don't get you," I say. "It's not like we haven't before."

"That was different."

"How?"

"Look, Bridget. Here's the thing. I like you. A lot. But—"

A hard lump wedges itself in my windpipe. "You can't break up with me," I say. "We were never really going out."

The confused look returns. "Break up with you?"

"I know that speech," I say. "I've *memorized* that speech. 'I like you, but I think we make better friends.'"

"Hey," he says. "Will you let me finish? I was saying that I like you—"

"But—"

"*But* you have some issues, some sort of unfinished business with your ex-boyfriend. I just . . . I don't want to get caught in the middle."

I say, "It's not like I still see him."

"You're not over him, though, and that's the problem."

"But I am," I say. "I mean, I think I am. And I like you, Jasper. I want to be with you. I'm *choosing* to be with you."

"You said 'sex,' Bridget. Is that what this is? Sex?"

I shake my head. "If it was about sex, we would've already done it again." Jasper looks at me blankly; I try again. "If it was about sex, it wouldn't have to be *you*."

He considers this a minute, head tilted slightly. My fingers stretch to a curl springing onto his forehead. His hair is thick and smooth and I honestly want nothing more at this moment than to touch the tip of my nose to the back of his neck.

My hand returns to my lap. I study it, noticing the chewed-off nails, the paper cut healing slowly in the crease of my left pointer finger, the dot of ink that's seeped into the skin between that finger and my thumb.

"I should go," I say after a while.

"Maybe. Maybe not."

Jasper cups my face in his palms, presses his lips against mine. There's no more talking, only kissing and touching and all the things that come easy to us. We fall back into the pillows, forgetting to turn out the lights.

FIFTEEN

THE PATTERN ESTABLISHES ITSELF RATHER QUICKLY, and I yield to the comfort of routine. Two nights a week, Jasper picks me up from work and we go for coffee at some other late-night establishment. Saturdays are dinner and a movie. Sundays we go to Pathmark and buy ingredients for whatever creation Jasper plans to cook that evening. We're disgusting in our domesticity.

Thanksgiving is approaching. Yesterday I told Fitzi I would dine with him and Katharine. The homemade-dinner idea was discarded instantly. My mother, he told me, will make reservations for us at the Green Room, host to a five-star buffet. "It's not exactly what I had in mind," he said. "But we'll be together, and that's what counts, right?"

Right.

Jasper is driving home for the long weekend. I know that

if I asked him, he'd stay in Newark with me, but that would mean subjecting him to dinner with Katharine, and I don't feel right inflicting her on anyone over the holidays. Still, we've already begun making plans for Christmas, New Year's, winter break. Jasper, it turns out, is quite the planner. It's nice, though. It gives me hope for the future—our future. And yes, I honestly believe we have a future together.

If my life were a made-for-TV movie, *this* would be its happy ending. But I stopped believing in happy endings years ago, when my parents divorced and my mom went psycho and my dad abandoned me and my boyfriend died.

I have to admit that things aren't always sunshine and roses in Twosville. Last week Jasper and I were running late to catch a movie at the Regal 16 and got stuck in bumper-to-bumper traffic. It took us nearly half an hour to inch a mile. Jasper, irritated, said something to the effect of "There better be a damn fine accident up ahead," and I completely freaked. I made him get off the highway at the next exit and drive me all the way back home on side streets. He kept asking me, "What? What did I say?" but my insides had gone all wobbly and I couldn't find my voice.

And that's the other thing: I still haven't come clean about Benji. Ellie thinks it's creepy that I've let Jasper believe Benji is merely an ex-boyfriend, and I don't know, maybe she's right. But whenever I make up my mind to tell him the truth, I think about how much time has gone by. How many opportunities I've let pass. Like when Jasper told me about his dad, who had a heart attack and died near the end of his freshman year in high school. I could've told him then, not just about Benji but also about my own fatherless existence. And yet the words wouldn't come, and so I think, *How can I tell him now?* If the situation were reversed and he were the one with this big secret he could've shared with me a zillion times over, I don't think I'd want to know.

At least, that's what I tell myself.

But then it happens. It's the Tuesday before Thanksgiving, the day before Jasper is set to drive home to New Jersey. We are eating dinner at the Bourbon Street Café, a place where Cajun cooking is served up with a massive helping of live jazz. All the elements are present—perfect gumbo, a dimly lighted dining room, and a tenor saxophone so low and mournful it tears all the way through me.

Tonight I will tell him everything.

We head back to the car. The air smells clean, like fresh laundry. Our arms are linked, and my head rests on his shoulder as we walk. I feel as if we're floating in a bubble built for two.

But then a third person appears, a tall blond woman with broad shoulders and an even wider stride. She shouts, "Do you believe in the power of love?" We stop, both of us looking over our shoulders at the same time, but there is no one else in the parking lot. "You," she yells, pointing at Jasper. "I'm asking you. Do you believe in the power of love?"

I stare at her, gripping Jasper's hand more tightly in mine, but he simply looks at me and says in a calm, even voice, "Always." The woman nods and resumes her brisk pace. I cannot remember experiencing a more surreal moment. I take it as a sign, as an affirmation that my decision to tell Jasper my story is spot-on.

Although it's going on ten, neither of us is very tired. Still, I'm itching to get back to my place—itching to finally break my silence. But first we must stop off at Jasper's Blockbuster to return the copy of *Annie Hall* he rented over the weekend. I plan to hop out of the truck and push the tape through the drop slot, but Jasper has a hankering for gummy worms and wants to go inside. So we do, and there, behind the counter, I see him.

Action Dan.

My chest gets tight, and gumbo-flavored bile gathers at the back of my throat as I feel the fragile walls of my couple bubble dissolve into the dry air. I duck behind a shelf of Sega games but it's too little too late. I've been spotted. I've been recognized. I've been . . . mistaken?

"Hey, Dan-o," Jasper says, approaching the counter.

"J-Dog, my man," Dan answers. "What up?"

Damn. Of course they know each other. Of course. I peer out at them from behind the shelter of Sega games as they chatter on in partially constructed sentences. Guy-speak. Jasper fidgets slightly, shifting his weight from one foot to the other. I see him crane his head some—looking for me, I presume. My pulse quickens, my breath catches in my throat. I can't hide here forever, but I'm thinking I can make it out the door unseen. Sucking in a deep breath, I poke my head around the shelf, trying to calculate the safest route when—

"There she is," Jasper says, waving me over. Meekly, I step toward the counter. Jasper slips his arm around my shoulders. "Dan, this is my girlfriend—"

"Bridget Edelstein," Dan says. "How you doin', girlie? I haven't seen you in forever. Not since—what? Graduation?"

"Yeah," I say. "Guess so."

Jasper offers me an amused look. "You know each other?"

I nod. "We went to Haley together."

"Me and the Bridge go way back." Dan's toothy grin fades. "Aw, dude, I'm sorry about Benji."

Here we go.

"It's okay," I say quickly.

"Naw, man," Dan continues. "That shit was *harsh*. I would've come home, you know, for the funeral? But I didn't find out for like two weeks after."

Jasper lets his hand slide to the spot between my shoulder blades, usually a comforting thing, but tonight his touch gives me chills. Dan rambles on, oblivious to the discomfort his words are causing. The anxiety steals my breath. My lungs scream for air.

"Listen," I say finally. "Great seeing you. But, uh, we have to run."

"Oh, yeah, yeah, of course," Dan says. He hastily scribbles his phone number on a New Releases flyer and makes me promise to call. We leave.

Back to the truck and painful silence. I wait for Jasper to say something—anything. It scares me, his not talking. Yelling—now that's a language I understand. But this doesn't translate. This doesn't compute.

"I was going to tell you," I say finally.

Jasper's eyes remain on the road. "Yeah?" he says, in the same calm, even voice I heard him use with the blond woman earlier. "When?"

"Tonight," I say. "I know you won't believe me, but it's true."

"Why do you say that?" His jaw is tight; his hands look superglued to the wheel. "Why don't you trust me?"

"I do," I say. "This isn't about you—it's about me. I—"

"You weren't ready," he interrupts. "I get it."

"Jasper—no. You don't." I can't look at him. I turn to the window before continuing. "He was never just my boyfriend—he was my . . . everything. My best friend. My *family*. And when we were together, it was like there was no me, no him—just us.

"But then he *died,* and it was gone—and everyone . . . They felt *sorry* for me. They looked at me like I was . . . I don't know . . . incomplete. Even Ellie." Here I pause, wipe some of the tears away. "I guess I was scared that if I told you, it would change the way you looked at me—the way you looked at *us*."

My eyes remain fastened on the world whirring by my window. I can't stop shivering.

And then I feel it. Jasper's hand. On the back of my head.

Stroking my hair, patting down the curls. A gesture so reassuring and tender that it breaks me. I drop my face into my palms and begin to sob.

Jasper eases the truck off into the emergency lane, puts it in park, and pulls me into his arms, into the warmth of his chest. "Shhh," he whispers. "It's okay, it's okay."

But it's not okay, not really, and before we even reach my place I know I will be sleeping alone tonight. So I'm not surprised when Jasper gently kisses my forehead and says, "We'll talk when I get back from break." He drives away before I've even walked through the front door, let alone locked it behind me.

Numb, I climb the stairs to the apartment. I crawl into my futon fully clothed, my legs curling into my stomach fetal-style. I think about our parking-lot prophet—"*Do you believe in the power of love?*"—and about how Jasper said "Always," but I said nothing, because I don't.

SIXTEEN

THANKSGIVING.

Full day ahead of me. First, pie-baking with Ellie, who offered to bring a Southern pecan deep-dish to her family's gathering, even though she's never made anything that wasn't boil-in-a-bag or microwave-ready. Then, on to the Green Room for Fitzi's family time. Finally, a stop at the Gilberts'. I hadn't planned to go there at all, but Mrs. Gilbert insisted. "You *will* come for dessert," she said firmly after I politely declined her dinner invitation. "You are family, Bridget, and that's what this holiday is all about."

Despite the fatigue that's enveloped me since Jasper's departure, I am grateful for the distraction. It keeps me from jumping every time the phone rings, from deflating when it isn't him. Why hasn't he called? I want to hear him say that he understands why I've kept quiet about Benji. Or maybe that he misses me and knows we can work though the mess I've made of things. He could've at least called just to say he'd gotten home safely.

He could've at least done that.

It is weirdly warm for a late-November morning, so my original choice of outfits—a cream-colored cashmere sweater set over a calf-length suede skirt in cranberry—is less than practical. Still, I didn't bother to have anything else dry-cleaned, so cashmere and suede it is. As I zip up my brown leather boots, the first beads of sweat spring up on my temples. I blot them with a liberal amount of pressed powder and pray that my makeup won't run before I see my mother.

Dressing for a visit with Katharine is an art. Her rules of aesthetics are complex and her eye misses nothing, especially where I am concerned. She has always felt a certain possessiveness about my body—what I put in it, what I do to it, what I dress it in. Once, when I was eleven, I asked her if I could get bangs. She said no and so I, stubborn girl that I was, chopped them myself with a pair of orange-handled kitchen scissors. Katharine screamed at me for two hours straight, cried the rest of the day, and refused to talk to or even look at me for at least a week.

What is it with the women in my life obsessing over my appearance? It's almost as bad as the men's proclivity for *dis*appearance.

———

I don't pull up to the Hotel Dupont until quarter past twelve, so I'm already fifteen minutes late—not an auspicious start. I hand the valet the keys to the Coach and rush into the Green Room through the glass doors.

The maitre d' leads me and my churning stomach to Fitzi and Katharine's table. Fitzi rises as I approach. Katharine is, as predicted, impeccably dressed: sleeveless black knit sweater over a sleek black skirt, the hemline of which hits right below her knees. I haven't seen her since her birthday in August, and in those three short months she looks as if she's dropped a good twenty-five pounds. She's so painfully thin that her pale skin looks almost translucent. As I lean to kiss her cool cheek, I smell her perfume, which reminds me of rotting roses soaked in Grand Marnier. "Hello, Mother."

"Was traffic bad?" she asks, checking her Movado watch.

"No," I say tightly. I turn to Fitzi, who gives me a big bear hug. "Car trouble." I'll say anything to avoid that woman's disapproval.

"Ah," Katharine says. I sit. Fitzi pulls a bottle of wine from a silver stand and pours some into my glass.

"Your mom let me order rosé—says it's becoming chic again." He throws a wink my way. I can't help grinning. Katharine fiddles with a corner of her freshly pressed linen napkin. After a few minutes of chitchat, she stands and says, "Shall we?"

We head to the buffet. Fitzi loads his plate: pecan-crusted salmon with a brandy-and-brown-butter baste, brussels sprouts with smoked bacon and pearl onions, roasted yams seasoned with fresh ginger and caramelized Vidalias. Katharine opts for a modest serving of braised lamb with currant dressing. I go for the turkey, dressed with a pine nut, sage, and corn bread stuffing. So much for Stove Top.

We keep our mouths full enough that real conversation isn't possible, at least not until Fitzi rises for seconds, stranding Katharine and me on an island of silence.

"So," she says.

"So," I say.

"How's work?"

"Fine."

"I see."

I can't remember the last time Katharine and I had a real conversation. We stopped talking when I turned sixteen and got my driver's license—my means of escape. Although, even then we argued. We had screaming matches that would leave our faces purple and our voices hoarse. It wasn't much, but at least we were honest in our hatred of each other.

Then came my overnight stay at the Christiana Hospital—the impetus for my sessions with Dr. Margie. Katharine didn't find out about it right away, not until the goons at the front desk decided to send my bill to Fitzi's place and not to my apartment as I had asked. Katharine, never shy about opening my mail, saw the five-hundred-dollar charge for the charcoal cocktail they made me drink to flush my system and went six degrees of spastic.

"Why were you in the hospital?" she demanded via cell phone. "Why were you kept for observation?"

"Ate some bad soy?" I joked halfheartedly. "Needed an alien probe removed?"

"I never thought you'd be capable of something so childish."

I laughed. "Come to think of it, wanting to die *is* sort of a goof, isn't it?"

The phone crackled. Katharine's stream of babble came through the line in short bursts. "You don't know from pain," I thought I heard her say just before we got disconnected. I slammed the receiver down and bit my hand until it bled.

"So I hear you're dating someone," Katharine says, swirling the wine in her glass.

"Who told you that?"

"Ellie. She called the house a few days ago, to wish me and Fitzi a happy Thanksgiving."

Note to self: Kill Ellie.

"Is it serious?" Katharine asks.

"Do you even care?"

Katharine's dark red eyelashes flutter together. "Of course I care."

"You don't have to lie, Mother. No one's around to hear you."

"Hate me if you must, Bridget," she says, draining her glass. "But remember this—I'm the only parent you've got."

Normally, this would be my cue to bolt. But the second I

throw my balled-up napkin on the table, Fitzi returns. "How are my girls doing?" he says, beaming at the two of us. I offer a weak smile. Katharine signals the waiter to bring another bottle of wine.

And so Fitzi eats, and Katharine drinks, and I pick at my ragged fingernails, and all is well in the Land of Make-Believe. This goes on for at least another hour before Fitzi slips the waiter his gold card. As he signs the receipt, he casually invites me to come back to the house, but I decline, offering a quick rundown of the rest of my day as an excuse, chasing that with a fairly hasty exit.

Or so I think. As I hand my ticket to the valet, Fitzi jogs toward me. "Glad I caught you, kiddo," he says, pulling on his charcoal-gray suit jacket. "Listen, I know you're busy and all, but it'd really mean a lot to your mom and me if you'd come over for a bit. Even an hour. Really."

"C'mon, Fitz—haven't I served my time?"

He frowns slightly. "Is that how you think of it?"

"It's not you," I sigh. "It's *her*."

Fitzi touches my arm lightly. "I don't know how to tell you this, Bridge, so let me just say it. Your mom's sick. Female stuff."

"What do you mean, 'female stuff'?"

"Polyps. They're not cancerous—not yet, anyway. But the doctors want to operate. They want to take it all out."

"A hysterectomy?" My voice, barely a whisper.

Fitzi nods. "It's been really hard on your mom. We've— well, we've been trying to have a kid for a couple years now.

I guess it just wasn't meant to be."

I don't even realize I'm crying until Fitzi's coarse thumb wipes some tears from my cheeks. "Why are you telling me this?" I ask.

"I thought you should know."

"No," I say. "Why are *you* the one telling me? Why isn't she? She's my *mother*."

"She's scared, kiddo."

The valet pulls my car up to the curb.

"I have to go," I say, not looking Fitzi in the eye.

"Bridge—"

"I'll call you later."

In my hurry to speed off to safety, I forget to apply the clutch. The car chokes and sputters, grinds to a halt. My seat belt tightens, cutting across my chest. I can't breathe, but it's not because of the seat belt. Anger and frustration surge through my body, down my arm and to the palm of my hand, which smacks hard against the steering wheel. *Goddamn her.* I never knew she wanted another me.

The attendant who greeted me when I first arrived at the Green Room approaches my car, taps on the glass. "Need help, miss?" he asks, soft and polite.

"No thanks," I say. "I think I can handle it on my own."

I drive away.

SEVENTEEN

THE FIRST THING I SEE when I pull up at the Gilberts' is the enormous For Sale sign staked in their front yard. At first I think it's a mistake, that the sign belongs to one of the neighboring town houses. But then I see a smaller sign hanging below: 18 CAPILANO ST.—AVAILABLE NOW!!!

I suppose deep down I knew this would happen eventually. All the grief books talk about being open to changing your environment—about how memorializing a home can't bring back the past, just keep the present from advancing to the future. Blah blah *blah*. Still, I can't believe they're actually trying to sell the place.

I can't deal. Not today. I slam the car into reverse and head back out onto Wilton. I'm racing toward 95 when my conscience gets the best of me. I can't just not show—I'm already forty minutes late. I pull into the 7-Eleven and hit the pay phone.

Mrs. Gilbert answers. "Where are you?"

"My mom's," I lie. "She, um, she's having surgery in a couple of weeks, and Fitzi asked me to spend the rest of the day with them."

She sighs. "I wish you'd come back."

"I'm sorry." If there is a train to hell, I bet I'm already booked on a Metroliner. "But it's my mom, you know?"

"Bridget—where are you calling from?"

"I—I told you," I stammer. "Mom's house."

"No," she says quietly. "I just saw you. Out the window."

Hanging up on her will hardly help my chances of avoiding the Hell Train. But I have no idea how to get myself out of this.

Mrs. Gilbert tosses me a line: "I suppose you saw the sign."

"Yeah," I say.

"Why don't you come back so we can talk about it?"

But I don't want to talk about it. I don't want put on the good-girl face, don't want to make nice with the assorted friends and family members assembled in the about-to-be-sold living room of the only real home I've ever known.

"I'm sorry," I say. "I can't."

"Fine." Mrs. Gilbert's voice has grown thin. "But, Bridget—I hope you realize you can't shut us out forever.

It won't make things easier. Not for you, and not for us. The good Lord doesn't want us to bear our burdens alone."

She hangs up without saying goodbye.

At home it is dark and quiet. Normally I like living alone—like having a protected space to myself; tonight, though, I wish I had company. I could call Ellie, see if she's back from her gram's house. But even if she is, Ellie's not the kind of person you can spill your guts to without judgment, and that's the last thing I need right now. The truth is, the only person I really want to talk to is Jasper, and it's fairly obvious he's skipped on to another wavelength entirely.

I turn on the TV, flip through the channels twice, turn it off again. Crack open a book, skim a few pages, close it a few minutes later. Smoke a couple of cigarettes, gnaw on half a bag of baby carrots, take a long shower. Finally, out of desperation, I call information for Garfield, New Jersey. There are more than thirty listings for Douglas, and I don't think Jasper's ever told me his mom's name. I thank the operator and put the phone back on its hook.

I could try going to sleep but it's barely seven. Why does my mother, who always treated me as if I was an inconvenience, suddenly want another child? And these polyps—how serious are they? I think about her catchphrase—"I'm the only parent you've got"—and can't decide whether to laugh or cry.

From the medicine chest in the upstairs bathroom, I pull out a vial of Xanax Katharine gave me not long after Benji died. "You'll need these," she said. "Think of them as your friends." For years she had offered me various combinations of pills to cure whatever she thought ailed me. Low-level amphetamines to speed up my metabolism. Steroid complexes to clear up my normal teenage skin. The Xanax to kill my anxiety. I had briefly considered downing them the night of my botched suicide attempt, but didn't want to leave Katharine awash in guilt, feeling as if she had loaded the gun herself.

I feel nearly as low tonight as I did then. Why? Why can't I get better? I can count the number of good days on one hand, and I know it shouldn't be this way. It shouldn't be this hard. Benji was my first love, but I doubt he'll be my last. Then again, maybe that's the point—that he *won't* be my last. Dr. Margie's always telling me I need to let myself mourn the loss of what could have been, not only with Benji but also with my father and Katharine. "Feeling sorry for yourself isn't mourning," she says. "And letting yourself experience pain is only the beginning."

The beginning of what, though? I'm tired of working so hard to feel even the teensiest bit good. What I need is a break. A vacation from myself. I open the vial, slide two blue pills into the palm of my hand, and gulp them down without water. Then I crawl into bed and wait for the numbing of my brain.

EIGHTEEN

Monday, eleven p.m.

Still no word from Jasper. He has to be back by now—he had P-chem this morning at nine and he never misses P-chem. I suppose I could call him—probably should—but part of me feels it's not my place.

I am tired of being the boy.

But by midnight I am a full-on basket case. I can't sleep, don't want to eat, and have had my fill of Nick at Nite reruns. Which is why, as the digital clock glows 12:27, I pull a pair of sneakers over my slipper socks, grab the keys to the Coach, and hit the door.

I smoke two whole Marlboros on the way to Jasper's dorm, despite the fact that it's barely an eight-minute drive. Shaking, I steer the car into a handicapped spot right outside the entrance, trying to forget that this is an insane hour for an unscheduled visit. Also that I'm wearing dirty flannel pajama bottoms and a T-shirt still bearing traces of a pizza I ate upwards of two weeks ago.

I buzz his room. No answer. I count to twenty, then buzz again. Still no answer. A minute goes by. I buzz a third time.

Finally, a response. "Yeah?"

"It's me," I say. "Bridget."

The lock clicks open. As I walk into the building, I realize I have no idea what comes next. My heart thumps like a tympani as I step lightly toward his room. The door is open; Jasper is hanging on the frame of it, wearing fuzzy plaid boxers and nothing else.

"Hey, you," he says, in a scratchy-sleepy voice. He plants a cold, dead kiss on my cheek, then backs into the room, flops back onto the bed.

I don't enter. Instead, I play Professor Duh: "Did I wake you?"

"Kinda," he says. "Yeah." Languidly, he scratches his naked belly, tucks his hand behind his tousled head. Totally casual, as if this is normal. As if we always go five days without talking. As if I routinely show up on his doorstep in the middle of the night. "So what's up?"

"When did you get back?" I ask.

"Last night."

"Oh." I swallow hard. "Did you have a good holiday?"

"Okay," he says. "You?"

So this is what we've come to. Polite chitchat. Why am I here? This isn't what I wanted. *He* isn't what I wanted.

117

"You didn't call," I say. My words come out a little too sharply. Fuck it. Fuck *him*.

"Yeah," he says. "I guess I should have. I just—I thought maybe you needed some space."

"Maybe you were the one who needed space."

"Maybe."

I shift my weight from foot to foot. Jasper sits up, gestures to his desk chair. I stay standing. I say, "So I guess it's over."

"Are you asking me or telling me?"

"I don't know. Asking."

"No," he says, arms crossed against his chest. "I don't think so."

This is . . . unexpected. My bottom lip quivers slightly. I will not cry. I will *not* cry.

Too late. "But you didn't call," I say.

Jasper stands, crosses to me. "I'm sorry," he says. "I should have called. I just—I didn't know what to say. Bad timing? I am sorry. Really."

But the waterworks are already flowing. Lately it's as though my emotions are too big for my body to handle, and they come shooting out like seltzer from a bottle that's been shaken. Snot drips from my nose onto Jasper's bare shoulder, but I'm crying too hard to care.

"I'm sorry too," I say between sobs. "For everything. All of it."

He pats my head and murmurs soothing words until I can rein in the tears. We sit on his bed. He catches both of my hands within his own. He pushes a few tear-dampened strands of hair away from my eyes. "You okay?"

I nod.

"So I did some thinking while I was away. And here's the thing: If we're going to make this work, you're going to have to start trusting me. I'm talking full disclosure. No editing the sad parts. And no thinking I'm going to bail at the first sign of discomfort, okay? Just because things get a little sticky doesn't mean I'll stop loving you."

And there it is. The *L* word.

"You love me?" I ask. I can't help it—I need to hear it again.

Jasper's eyes narrow slightly. "You know that," he says. "Don't you?"

I shake my head.

"Jesus, Bridge—What do you think we've been doing the past few months? Playing house?"

"I don't know."

"Look—I know none of this makes sense. I know the laws of logic dictate that I never should've found out your name, let alone taken you on a proper date. But screw logic. This is good. *We're* good. Aren't we?"

I lift my eyes to meet his. They're so beautiful, his eyes. "You talk like a girl," I say.

Jasper laughs, a clear, throaty laugh. "Oh, yeah? So what's that make you?"

"Happy."

NINETEEN

WE KISS FOR A WHILE, and then talk for a while, and then there's more kissing and then more talking. Actually, I do most of the talking. I tell Jasper as much as he—strike that, as much as I—can handle, beginning with the Benji stuff and finishing with Katharine's impending surgery. Jasper, an active listener, nods and asks questions in appropriate places. He can also sense when I'm disclosing something particularly difficult, and it is in those moments that his eyes get soft and he brushes his hand across a patch of my skin screaming for human contact.

"You're so strong," he says, playing with my fingers. "Your bones are so small, so fragile, but you're so damn strong. What's your secret? What makes you so *you*?"

I talk until my voice takes on the raspiness of a three-pack-a-day smoker. My confession peters out around sunup, when the two of us pass out from sheer exhaustion, my head tucked close to Jasper's, his arm snaked across my waist.

The alarm goes off around eight; after hitting Snooze six or seven times, Jasper decides to blow off classes and falls back asleep. I follow suit and don't regain consciousness until well after one. My body feels like perfectly cooked spaghetti, all loose and languid. I can't remember the last time I woke up feeling this refreshed.

And then it hits me: For the first time in nearly ten months, I didn't dream about Benji. In fact, I'm pretty sure I didn't dream at all.

Beside me, Jasper sleeps on, and I watch him for a while. He looks as peaceful as I feel. I run my finger down the side of his slightly stubbly cheek, tracing an imaginary line from his ear to his neck, over his shoulder and along his taut, muscled arm. His mouth is parted a bit, allowing a small sigh of a snore to escape every few breaths, and I want to trace the line of his lips, too, but I don't want to wake him just yet. There is light, fluttery movement behind his eyelids. It makes me wonder what he's dreaming.

Minutes crawl by before Jasper shows signs of stirring. He rubs his eyes with his fists, smiles sleepily, pulls me closer. I feel—dare I think it?—*safe*. We cuddle for a few minutes before he declares a need for food. He loans me his DU sweatshirt to cover my crusty T. It's not until we're deciding which car to take that I remember I parked the Coach in a handicapped spot. Sure enough, there are three

(three!) tickets jammed under the windshield wiper. I drive, if only to escape certain towing.

We cruise across the Maryland state line, to the Waffle House across the street from the Skillet. Chuck, my manager, would kill me if he knew about my surreptitious visits here, as the smallish diner has co-opted some of our business in recent months. But nobody can turn a mound of hash browns like the Waffle House folks.

We slide into a corner booth and place our order. Jasper digs some stray quarters from the pocket of his jeans and heads to the jukebox. As he plunks in his selections, he turns and offers me the most scrumptious of grins. It's strange how quickly your entire life can change; just twenty-four hours ago, I was crawling deeper and deeper into the Hole, sure that Jasper had chucked me for good. And now today, everything seems so new, so full of possibility. I think of how badly I treated him in the beginning, how far I kept trying to push him away, and how he sucked it up, rode it out—how he never once doubted the rightness of us. His tenacity amazes me.

And even though I don't really believe in God or any sort of higher power, I find myself saying a silent prayer of thanks, right there in the vinyl Waffle House booth, to whoever or whatever made this all happen.

After we eat, Jasper picks up the check and heads to the register. As he counts out a fistful of ones, I say, "Feel like taking a ride?"

"Sure," he says. "Where to?"

"You'll see."

It's a perfect late-fall afternoon—cloudless ice-blue sky, crisp but gentle breeze. We crack the windows, light some cigs, and blare a tape of old-school Beasties. Jasper fiddles with the controls on my radio. "How 'bout a little bass?" he shouts, turning it up full-throttle.

I grin. "Rock on."

We vibrate up 273, through Hares Corner and straight into Old New Castle. It's like going through a time warp: old mom-and-pop stores, the brick courthouse, and to our left, one spindly cobblestone street. I park the Coach by the wharf, unsnap my seat belt. "We're here."

"Where's here?"

"Duh," I say. "Battery Park."

We hit the pavement, follow the sidewalk that winds along the water. I point out my favorite bench. "If you sit there at night and imagine that bridge thing is the mast of a boat, it looks just like a van Gogh painting." We press on. I point out the Fool-on-the-Hill hill, named after I caught a Beatles documentary on PBS that had footage of Paul flailing about on a similar slope of grass as the eponymous song played.

I show Jasper my favorite willow tree, stripped of all greenery and looking sadder than usual. "That's the picnic tree," I say. "There's a knot in the wood—it kind of sticks out like a shelf—and we'd always put the radio there."

"Who's we?"

"Oh," I say. "Me and Benji."

"I see."

I take Jasper's hand, pull him toward the swings. He plops into a low red one, drags his feet in the rust-colored dirt. "So why'd you bring me here?" he asks.

"I don't know. I guess—this place means a lot to me. Lot of memories."

"Benji memories?"

"Some," I say, embarrassed. "Not all."

He nods as if he understands, but there's now a palpable awkwardness hanging over us. We fake-swing in silence. After a few minutes, Jasper jumps off, starts walking away.

"You okay?"

He jams his hands into his pockets. "Not really."

"What's wrong?"

Jasper shrugs. "I guess I don't get it. You and this place, bringing me here. It's like—I don't know."

"What?" I prod.

"It's my fault," he says, staring into the sun, his eyes gone all hard and squinty. "I should've known I couldn't compete with the dead guy."

Insert pin-drop silence.

The irritation melts from Jasper's face, leaving it clean, blank, frozen. Scared.

I swallow hard. "I can't believe you just said that."

Jasper's eyes drop to the ground. "I'm sorry, Bridge. I don't—Christ, I'm so sorry. You know I didn't mean it. You know that."

He reaches out to me, but I turn away, heading toward the car. I hear the crunch of dead twigs behind me. I speed up, break into a run. Jasper calls out to me, but I ignore him, running the full length of the park. When I reach the Coach, my face bears a slight film of sweat.

Jasper slows as he approaches. "Please," he says. "I'm sorry."

I ignore him and climb into the driver's seat. After hesitating for a minute, I unlock the other door.

Jasper says nothing as I speed back to Newark. Finally, I pull into the lot outside his dorm. He opens his door but doesn't move.

"Get out," I say.

"Bridget—*please*."

"Go."

He goes. I stare at him hard, trying to shrink him with my eyes. My breath comes in short, quick bursts. I cannot move. Jasper places one hand on the passenger-side window. His movement jerks me back into the moment. I can feel every nerve in my body bristle underneath my skin. He stands there, still frozen. Looking so little. So lost.

Looking as if *I'm* the one who hurt *him*.

I press my foot on the gas, hard, and squeal onto the street.

──────── TWENTY ────────

THE DAYS THAT FOLLOW ARE FAIRLY QUIET. Jasper leaves a couple of bland messages—"Bridge, it's me. Give me a call when you get a chance"—which I, of course, do *not* return. I'm not trying to punish him. I'm not even that mad anymore. It's just—it's not what I expected. These messages—which I assume are feeble attempts to apologize—seem so . . . *small*.

I want passion. I want grand romantic gestures. I want John Cusack standing outside my bedroom window, a portable radio hoisted high above his head, blaring our song. Not this. Not "*Call me when you get a chance.*" As if his bad behavior has forced me to fill my calendar with a whirl-wind of social engagements.

It's funny; after Benji died, all I wanted was to be left alone. But now it's different. Now I actually *want* someone to find me here crying. Ask me what's wrong. Ask me how they can fix it, what they can do to make it better. I know that's not the way life works. If I've learned anything from Dr. Margie, it's that change, real change, must come from within. But I don't know how to fix this myself. I don't know how to make it better.

I'm not even a hundred percent sure I know what's wrong.

Friday sneaks up on me. I'm scheduled to work three to ten at the Skillet, but when I arrive, Chuck tells me that Darlene, who works midnight to seven, has called in sick. He asks me if I can pull a double and cover for her, and I say yes, if only to have something with which to fill the time. Chuck beams proudly; I was his first new hire as manager and I'm one of the only young waitresses he's managed to keep for more than six months.

By the time I finish the second shift, I'm wiped. After steeling myself with yet another cup of caffeine, I drag my body to the Coach and head for home. I'm so tired, I'm actually looking forward to sleep. But I've barely locked the front door behind me when the phone rings. I race to catch it, thinking it might be Jasper, and swoop the receiver up to my ear.

Anna.

"Hi," she says, sniffling loudly. "It's me."

"Are you okay?"

"Can you come over here? Like *right now*? Please?"

Without a pause I say, "Sure. Just tell me what's wrong."

"The *tree*," she wails. "They're making me go with them to get the *tree*."

"I'll be right there."

Despite my near-exhaustion, or maybe because of it, adrenaline kicks me into gear. I race to the Gilberts' house in record time, cursing at red lights and chain-smoking to calm my tissue-paper nerves. How could I have forgotten the tree? The annual trip to Miller's Tree Farm had been Benji's favorite thing about Christmas, the only family tradition in which he was a willing participant. I'd heard about the annual excursion for years, but hadn't been invited along until last December—by his mother, no less—three weeks after Benji had sent the breakup letter, but before he had gotten around to telling his parents about the split.

"Let's just get through this," Benji said dully, jaw tight, shoulders stiff. "But after Christmas . . ." I nodded, trying to stuff my smile behind a blank, plastic face. *At least we have Christmas,* I thought. *Maybe New Year's, too.* And then, after I'd made Benji remember what good times we always had together, maybe then he'd decide it was stupid, that he'd acted too quickly, and we could go back to being what we had been.

At Miller's, we all boarded the hay wagon that took us to the heart of the tree grove. Benji sat stiffly, fingering the buttery leather sheath that covered his small ax. The hood of his bright red sweatshirt hid most of his little-boy face. With the pungent smell of pine filling my nostrils, I took his cold, unmittened hand in mine. Though he flinched, he didn't pull away.

Starkly determined, Benji crept silently through the grove, scouting trees stealthily, as if they would run away. "Too tall," he muttered occasionally. Or, "Look at this fat thing. Hey, Papa, should we put it out of its misery?" Finally, he settled for a prim pine with stiff branches. "This is it," he said. "This is the one."

As I watched him take the first swing, arms strong and sure and steeled for the resistance of the tough bark, my body flooded with love. *Look at him,* I thought. *Look at my Benji.* I fantasized about the time when we would be his parents' age, when we would load our three children into our own minivan and drive an hour past the Maryland state line to the Miller's lot. It never occurred to me that the breakup letter was real. I thought it was just a phase he was going through, like his brief flirtation with Buddhism back in the ninth grade or his short-lived obsession with gangsta rap his junior year.

My queasiness grows as I press the ancient doorbell. There is a SOLD! banner crossing the For Sale sign to my right. That was quick. I ring again; this time Mr. Gilbert answers. He waves me in. Automatically, I slip off my wet shoes, hang my charcoal coat on the third peg from the right. In the living room, I hear Anna's tantrum raging on: "No! You can't make me go!"

"She's here," Mr. Gilbert announces in his stale, solemn way. Anna rushes into the foyer, where I stand frozen.

"Bridget, oh my God," she says, hurling herself into my arms. "They won't make me go if you tell them not to. Tell them I don't have to, please!"

Mrs. Gilbert thumps into the foyer. "Why don't you two go up to Anna's room and have a talk? We'll leave in half an hour."

Upstairs, Anna's chin quivers and she starts to cry again. "I'm sorry," she says, over and over. "I'm so sorry."

"For what?"

"I know I'm acting like a baby."

"No, you're not," I say, smoothing strands of blond hair from her puffy face.

"I miss him so much," she says. "I don't want it to be Christmas. It doesn't feel like Christmas, not with him . . . gone."

"I know."

"I know you know—that's why I called you. So why don't *they* know that?"

I sigh, pulling Anna's cold hands into my own. "They do. Why do you think they're selling the house? Your parents— they're doing what they can. They're trying."

"Trying to forget," she says.

"No," I say. "They can't forget him any more than you or I can. I think they're trying to put it all back together. You have to let go before you can hold on."

We sit silent for a while. Anna pulls pieces of fuzz off her worn chenille bedspread and places them in a small, neat pile by her left knee. When the pile grows to the size of a Ping-Pong ball, she lets out a heavy sigh. "I don't want to forget him."

"Me either," I say. "And neither do they."

Anna nods, sweeps the pile of fuzz balls onto the floor. "Will you come?" she asks. "I think I can do this if you're there."

My throat grows tighter, my skin colder. "I don't know," I say. "This is kind of a family thing."

"But you *are* family," Anna says. "Sisters, no matter what, right?" Her blue eyes cut straight through me. Sapphire eyes, slightly smaller, slightly softer, but Benji's nonetheless. I look into them with a strange mixture of fear and sadness, knowing Anna is right. Knowing this will never be over, I'll never be completely free.

"Sisters," I say, rising. "Well, come on, then. Let's just get through this."

TWENTY-ONE

WE PILE INTO THE VAN. Anna, exhausted from her lengthy crying jag, promptly falls asleep on my shoulder. Charlie curls up on my other side and does the same. Mrs. Gilbert pops in a tape of John Denver singing Christmas carols with the Muppets but keeps the volume low. From time to time, I catch her mouthing the words, but Mr. Gilbert's disapproving looks stop her before any audible notes escape her lips. It's not long before she turns the music off altogether.

We arrive at the tree farm and are shuttled onto a hay-lined truck bed. The heavy wind blows so hard that the brief hayride seems to last for hours. Anna clutches my hand with both of hers, holding on as tightly as she did at the funeral nearly a year ago. I kiss her temple and try to think of soothing things to say, but nothing comes to mind.

One step forward, two steps back.

Hours later, after we find a tree and return to the house, Mrs. Gilbert dumps some premade stew into a large pot and begins chopping vegetables for a salad. "You'll stay for dinner," she says to me, more of a command than a request. I nod, then duck into the den and call the Skillet to let them know I won't be in. "Family emergency," I say when Chuck asks me why. He isn't pleased, but there's not much he can do, considering my heroic double shift last night.

Without any prompting, Charlie sets the table, careful to put the spoons on the right side and forks on the left. Anna and I cuddle on the overstuffed couch in the den, watching reruns of *The Waltons* on the Family Channel. Mr. Gilbert stays alone in the living room, screwing the spruce into a rusty tree stand as his wife works on her salad. It's so right.

It's all wrong.

"I'm glad you're here," Anna says after a while.

"Me too," I lie.

"I feel like I never see you anymore."

I nod. "Yeah, I know."

"It's okay, though. I understand. I mean, I wouldn't be here either, if I didn't have to be."

"Anna—"

"Don't," she says. "Don't 'Anna' me like you don't know what I'm talking about." She turns toward me, eyes wide, searching. "You *do* know, don't you?"

"Yes," I say. "I know."

"Dinner!" Mrs. Gilbert trills. We shuffle to the chipped faux-wood dining room table and sit in our respective seats:

Anna to the left of Mrs. Gilbert, who sits at the head; me to Mrs. Gilbert's right. Mr. Gilbert takes the foot, and Charlie slides in next to Anna. Benji's place, the one between me and Mr. Gilbert, remains empty. Nothing, not even a serving dish, is ever put on the vinyl place mat that rests in front of what's still his chair. It's as if there's an invisible force field around the space—a Benji buffer zone. Even I don't let my elbows enter the off-limits territory.

"Bridget," says Mr. Gilbert, after clearing his throat. "Would you like to say grace?" He flashes me a weak and watery smile, nearly a smirk. No, of course I wouldn't like to say grace—which is exactly why he's asked me.

"I'll do it!" Charlie pipes in. I love that kid. "I'll say grace."

"No, Charlie. Bridget's our guest. I'm sure she'd love to—"

"*Richard,*" Mrs. Gilbert cuts in sharply. "Bridget is *hardly* a guest. And in all the hundreds of dinners she's eaten here has she ever taken you up on your offer? Stop tormenting the poor girl and let Charlie say the prayer."

By the time we finish dessert—a fresh-baked apple brown Betty—my eyes are so raw and swollen that I'm sure they're about to pop out of my skull. I haven't had a lick of sleep in the last forty hours, and my head is so woozy I feel as if I've downed a bottle of Nyquil and chased it with a shot of whiskey.

I begin to say my goodbyes when Mrs. Gilbert asks me to help her carry some laundry into the basement. "I really have to go," I say.

Mrs. Gilbert smiles patiently. "It will only take a minute."

She wins.

I hoist myself up to sit on the freezer unit and bite my cuticles as Mrs. Gilbert sorts her colors from her whites. "Is something bothering you, Bridget?" she asks.

There are a zillion things bothering me at this moment: Katharine's coldness, Jasper's heartlessness, Benji's lifelessness. And yet, offering any one of these as an answer means allowing Mrs. Gilbert access to the parts of myself I try to keep hidden from her. So I decide to deflect attention to a common target: her husband.

"Why does Mr. Gilbert still hate me?" I say. "At least before, it sort of made sense. But now that Benji—now that he's gone, it seems silly. You know?"

"Is that what you think? That he hates you?" She smiles as if something I've said amuses her.

"Yes."

She shakes her head. "He doesn't hate you, dear. He's jealous of you."

"How so?"

Mrs. Gilbert carefully measures purplish detergent into its cap, then pours it over the clothes in the machine and presses Start. "You know Benji always put up his guard around us. He never talked to us, unless he was making a joke." She turns to face me. "He was different with you, though. *You,* he trusted. You knew him in a way that we never will. What parent *wouldn't* be jealous?"

And even though she doesn't say it, I see in her eyes, now

slightly narrowed, that she shares Mr. Gilbert's envy. The damp basement air stings the back of my throat. I don't know how to respond. It's not as if I've done anything wrong.

She returns to the laundry, then says, "There's a reason I asked you down here. I need a favor." She pauses dramatically, then continues. "We're moving at the beginning of February, and I've got to get this house in shape. There's more than fifteen years' worth of clutter to sort through—I'm hoping to get rid of all the nonessentials as quickly as possible."

"Oh," I say, relieved. "Sure. I can help you pack."

"Of course, any help you offer is much appreciated. But there's a specific task I had in mind for you."

Uh-oh.

"Don't," I say.

"He wouldn't want us going through his things."

"He wouldn't want me going through them either."

"Nonsense," she says. "You're the only person Benji would trust."

Before I can stop myself, I blurt out, "We broke up, you know. Two months before the accident." Her eyes widen; she doesn't even try to mask her surprise. "It's true," I continue. "Really."

She turns her attention to the dryer, pulling out armfuls of socks and underwear. "It wouldn't have lasted," she says. "You would've gotten back together."

Why would she say that? Even if it's true—and I don't

think it is—why would *anyone* say that? It doesn't fix anything. It doesn't bring him back.

"I won't do it," I say. "His room—I won't. It's not right, and you know it."

Mrs. Gilbert smiles patiently. "Let's discuss it later."

Silence fills the basement. I can barely keep my eyes open. *Yawn.* The noise startles Mrs. Gilbert. She asks me what's wrong. I tell her about the double shift—about how I haven't slept in almost two days—and the mother hen's feathers ruffle. She says, "I can't let you drive, then. You'll sleep here tonight."

I try to protest but it's no use. When it comes to things like this, Mrs. Gilbert gets what Mrs. Gilbert wants. She disappears into a storage closet and pops back out carrying an old Star Wars comforter and two flattened pillows.

"Hey," I say. "I know it's a tight fit at the inn, but do you expect me to camp out on the basement floor?"

"Don't be silly." She gestures to the left—toward Benji's room. "There's a perfectly good bed right in there."

The sickness in my stomach grows. "You can't be serious."

She scuttles past me, spreading the comforter over Benji's water bed, pretending she hasn't heard me. Is she on crack? I cannot believe she really expects me to sleep on that thing.

"I'm leaving," I say.

"No, you're not." She grabs my arm, not roughly, but with a firmness I know I don't have the strength to fight. Numb, queasy, I slip into the familiar squish of the water bed. The pillowcases smell like Downy. Mrs. Gilbert kisses my forehead, wishes me sweet dreams, and leaves me to the darkness. I figure I'll lie here until I hear her and Mr. Gilbert head upstairs for the night, then sneak out the front door. Only, the sleep monster steals my consciousness before I finish plotting my escape.

TWENTY-TWO

WHEN I WAKE UP, it's still dark. Then again, I *am* in a basement. I turn on the desk lamp, clipped to a thin section of the headboard, wipe some sleep from my eyes, and scan the room for a clock. Nothing. There's a cardboard chest of drawers next to the bed, and automatically, I yank open the top one and start feeling around for the pocket watch. It's still there. My hand closes around its smooth metal casing, and with a few wiggles, I'm sitting up on the slightly undulating mattress.

I don't open the pocket watch right away. Instead, I turn it over, run my fingers over the engraving on the back. *To B-man, With Love Always, Bridget*. I bought it for his sixteenth birthday after hearing him admire the one Fitzi always carried—a polished brass antique that Fitzi's grandfather had passed down through the firstborn boys. Benji ate that watch with his eyes, asked to hold it, swinging it slightly by the S chain looped through the top hook, looking like a misplaced silent-movie star. It surprised me, how clearly he loved that watch. He'd never been big on possessions. At any rate, I looked at him with the watch and knew he had to have one of his own.

I searched for weeks, taking a Polaroid of Fitzi's watch with me, trying to find something the least bit similar. I combed pawnshops, did the flea market circuit, bid crazy amounts of cash on eBay. Finally, just three days before Benji's birthday, I found *the* watch. It wasn't old, and it didn't come with the deceptively fine S chain, but it was heavy and round and matte, and it had an inky blue face with delicate yet manly hands that moved in effortless sweeping motions. It cost more than anything I'd ever purchased in my entire life—$270, plus extra for the rush engraving job—but it was so perfect, I just knew he'd love it.

Benji opened the package quickly, not waiting until we got to the restaurant, shredding the expensive gold paper and dropping it on the floor of the car. I couldn't see his face as he lifted the top off of the box, but I could feel the disappointment. "Wow," he said. "You spent too much." I wanted to cry.

"I thought you wanted one," I said.

"I did."

"There's something on the back of it."

"I saw."

"You hate it."

"No," he said. "Thanks."

Later, after a mostly silent dinner at La Tolteca, I drove to the park and we walked its perimeter. Before we finished the first lap, I felt an ache in my chest—a throbbing emptiness between my ribs. I stopped, reached for Benji's arm. "Would you have liked it better in silver?"

"It's not that," he said. "It's too nice. I've never owned something so nice."

"I'm not supposed to give you nice things?"

Benji sighed heavily.

I said, "I put a lot of thought into that watch."

"I know."

"So can't you just be happy?"

He didn't answer. When we got back to his house, he slipped the watch into the top drawer of the cardboard chest and never talked about it again. Apparently he didn't even think to take it with him when he went off to school. The California stuff was shipped back in two tall cartons and his steamer trunk, all resting in the back corner of the basement, all untouched. Strange that the Gilberts never went through the contents, never wanted to see what took up space in Benji's world in the last days before he died. Or maybe it isn't so strange after all.

If the watch is right, it's barely four-thirty A.M. Too early to be finished sleeping, too late to call it a nap. I don't want to be here anymore. I put the pocket watch back in the drawer, shut it, and tiptoe up the stairs. I scrawl a quick note to Mrs. Gilbert—*Feeling better, going home, thanks for everything, B.*—and slip out the door.

Seeing the pocket watch—remembering its story—brings up so much of the frustration I've worked so hard to bury. All I wanted to do was make Benji happy, and nothing I did made him happy enough. Or maybe I did too much, and that's the point.

I need to talk. I need to empty the contents of my brain into someone else's. I need Ellie.

It would make sense for me to go home, get some more sleep, and call her at a respectable hour, but I don't want to wait. So I head up Route 13, stopping at the twenty-four-hour Wawa for a cup of coffee and a bagel. I park in front of Ellie's house around five, eat my breakfast, and smoke until I can't take it anymore.

The neighbor's poodle *yip-yips* as I sneak around the side of the house and rap my knuckles on Ellie's bedroom window. It takes a while to rouse her—she's such a heavy sleeper—but when I finally do, she's surprisingly understanding. She lifts the glass and says, "Bridget, what's wrong?"

"Got a minute?" I ask.

I brace myself for some snide comment about the time, or some overly dramatic remark like "You didn't try to . . . *you know*—did you?" But all Ellie does is nod, motion me around, and unlock the front door.

I sit quietly at the small oak table in the Petersons'

kitchen as Ellie scoops some Maxwell House French Roast into an old coffeemaker. As it brews, she serves up two thick slices of crumb cake, then sets out a couple of bowl-sized cappuccino mugs. Wordlessly, she pours three scoops of sugar and a generous dose of half-and-half into mine, then pops it in the microwave for exactly twenty-two seconds— long enough to take the chill off but just shy of forming a skin on top of the liquid. I've forgotten how nice it is to be with someone who knows about things like drink preferences without asking. When the Mr. Coffee belches the last drops of caffeine, Ellie fills both our mugs and settles in across from me.

I take a stiff swig and sigh in appreciation. "You're so good to me."

"I try." She pops a pinch of crumb cake into her mouth, pushes some sleep-smushed hair out of her eyes, and says, "So what's up?"

I haven't really talked to Ellie since the Ceremonial Burning of the Sweatpants, so it takes another mug of coffee and two more squares of crumb cake to bring her up to speed. I pause at times, waiting for her to break in with some patented I-can-fix-your-life advice, but surprisingly, none comes. Even when I feel my eyes fill up with tears, she doesn't say a word, just fetches me a box of Kleenex.

"Well," she says once I've finished. "Talk about intense."

I apologize for waking her up at such an insane hour, but she waves me off. "Jesus, Bridge—how much is one person expected to take? And his *mother*. How creepy is she?

Making you sleep in that bed. You'd think she'd have a little sensitivity."

"She's lost it," I say. "Do you know she still hasn't gone through the cartons of stuff his school sent back? I mean, hasn't even opened the boxes."

"Yet she expects *you* to pick through the contents of an entire room. That's lovely." Ellie divides the last of the crumb cake and rises to make another pot of coffee. "So what are you gonna do?"

"About what?"

"The Gilberts. Jasper. Your mom."

I shake my head. "I have no idea."

"Look," she says, plopping back into her chair. "I know you hate unsolicited advice, but if it were me dealing with all this, I'd have to do some prioritizing. Katharine's always been a lost cause, so I say tackle her last. Stalling the Gilberts should be pretty easy—just tell them you'll help them out once the holidays are over."

"And Jasper?"

"That's a toughie. On one hand, it was a pretty schmucky thing he said. But on the other, you're right—he *has* stuck it out. And I could be wrong, but it sounds like you're pretty crazy about this guy."

"Sometimes," I say. "Sometimes not so much."

Ellie sweeps the remaining cinnamon crumbs dotting her plate into her coffee mug, stirs them around with her pinkie finger. "I think the real problem is that you somehow feel like you're cheating on Benji, or even his *family*, by letting yourself fall for someone else. Which is silly, really. You're not Scarlett O'Hara. No one will condemn you if you want to dance at the party."

"I just wish it wasn't so hard. You know?"

"Please. When is it *not* hard? Life isn't a date movie, and it never will be. All relationships take effort."

"Even friendships," I add.

"Yes," she says. "Even those."

TWENTY-THREE

I KNOW IT SOUNDS CORNY, but I leave Ellie's feeling like a brand-new Bridget. Like a superhero version of me. Able to leap chemically imbalanced parental units and loopy ex-future-mothers-in-law in a single bound. More importantly—*most* importantly—I finally feel ready to make peace with my boyfriend.

My boyfriend. I can't believe how strange it is, still, to think of Jasper that way. But he *is* my boyfriend, and he *does* love me, and when I can shut off my internal censor for more than a minute, I realize that I kind of love him, too. I've never told him that, though, and I need to.

I call him the minute I get home, but he's not in, and I don't really want the first time I say "I love you" to be via voice mail. I leave a short message, take a long, hot shower, and pop in a video while I wait for him to call me back.

I'm so intent on the movie that it's almost ten before I realize there may be a reason Jasper hasn't returned my call. I figured he was spending the day sequestered in the library—not out of the ordinary for him and his chemical-engineering brethren—but now I'm not so sure. Maybe he's already gotten my message and is now blowing me off in retaliation for my blowing him off earlier this week.

There's one way to find out. I dial his number. The voice mail picks up again, and while I'm debating whether or not I should leave a second message, my doorbell rings. I hang up and race down the stairs.

Jasper.

"Hi," I say.

"Hey," he says.

"I guess you got my message."

"Yeah," he says. "I did."

"You want to come in?" I ask.

"Not really."

"Oh."

In my superhero state of mind, I didn't stop to think our reconciliation could be so awkward. Worse, I never considered the possibility that there might be no reconciliation this time. I step out on the front porch, pulling the door closed behind me.

Jasper fumbles around in the pocket of his jeans. "I made you something," he says, handing me what looks like a tiny pad of Post-It notes.

"You made me office supplies?"

"No, silly. Look closer."

If he's calling me "silly," it can't be all that bad. I dip my head to better examine the Post-Its. In the dim orangey glow of my porch bug light, I see there are tiny pictures inked on each leaf of the pad, like one of those souvenir flip books you see at the Disney store. I fan the pages with my thumb and watch as a little stick dude picks up a frying pan, whacks himself on the head with it, and shouts, "I'm sorry!" in big bubble letters. I run the "movie" three more times before I'm able to look Jasper straight in the eye, but even so, I'm not prepared for the sad-puppy look on his face.

"You didn't have to do this," I say.

"I know."

"Let me finish. You didn't have to do this because you're not the one who needs to apologize."

His eyes squinch up as if I'm speaking Polish. Impulsively, I reach for his hand. He flinches, but I don't let go. "I took you to the park that day because it was the setting for nearly every meaningful experience I had in my adolescence, and I wanted to share that part of myself with you. I guess I never stopped to think that it might make you uncomfortable. And I should have."

"Maybe," he says. "But I was the one acting like some jealous caveman."

"You know what? We could apologize to each other all night and it's not going to change anything."

Jasper wriggles his hand from my grasp. "So why did you call me?"

"Let me finish," I say again. "We can't change the things we've said and done, but we *can* try to change the things we say and do from now on. Are you sure you don't want to come in? It's kind of cold out here." Jasper shakes his head. I ask him if we can at least walk, and he nods. "I've been thinking about what you said—about not being able to compete with Benji—and the thing is, you're right. You can't compete. Not because you're not as good as he was, and not because my feelings for you aren't as strong, but because it's not a competition. I think that's the mistake we've both been making—thinking that it is."

He says nothing, and I'm running out of words. We've walked the full circle of my driveway. Jasper stops and sits on the curb, and I follow suit. He lights two cigarettes and hands one to me, and we sit smoking in silence while silver puffs dance around our heads. Jasper, illuminated by a too-large moon and set against an incredible backdrop of inky blue, looks more beautiful to me than anything I've seen in a long, long time.

"Why do we smoke?" he wonders aloud. "I mean, it's this stupid, pointless act that does bad things to our bodies. So why do we do it?"

Talk about non sequiturs. I shrug. "They say it's the only acceptable form of suicide."

"They? Which 'they' is that?"

"I don't know. Vonnegut, I think."

"Is that why you smoke?"

I shake my head. "I think it's the breathing, really. Conscious breathing. Breathing for a reason."

Jasper laughs. "Life-affirming suicide. I like that."

And I'm not sure why I choose this moment, but I say, "You know, I once downed an entire bottle of over-the-counter pain reliever."

"For sport?"

"Not exactly." I look away. "It was like five months after Benji died. Everything just hurt too much, you know? I didn't know if I could do it anymore."

Jasper stubs out his cigarette with his boot. "So what happened?"

"I tucked myself into bed and waited awhile. Then I had this panic attack because I was sure no one would find me in time. And that's when I realized I wanted to be found. So I got dressed and drove to the emergency room. They made me drink a cup of liquid charcoal. I shit black for days."

He stifles a chuckle. "No, it's okay," I reassure him. "It's funny to me now. I mean, it really was this pathetic, half-hearted attempt."

A new, less comfortable silence sets in. Jasper reaches for my hand, but he keeps staring into the distance. "What are you thinking?" I ask him, not entirely sure I want to know.

Without missing a beat, he says, "Was it really as good as you remember?"

I sigh. "I don't know, Jasper. I know I loved him. And I think, in his own way, he loved me, too."

"That's not what I asked you."

Jasper's eyes are now focused on my mouth. It's making me feel itchy. "I don't know what you want me to say. It was good, and then it wasn't, and then it was over, and then it wasn't . . . and then he died."

"Fair enough," he says. "Can I ask you another question?"

"You just did."

"What do you miss most about him?"

I shrug.

"C'mon," he says. "You can do better than that."

A small sigh escapes me. I run my tongue over my chapped lips. "There's no one big thing," I say. "I miss the way he'd beam at me when I'd made a funny joke. Or the way other people would look at me when they'd see us together. Even before he took on the title of boyfriend, everyone knew I was his girl. And I liked that. I liked the idea of belonging to someone else. Does that make sense?"

"Yeah," he says. "Yeah, it does."

Jasper touches his pointer finger to my bottom lip. Then he turns so that his face is in my hair, his nose to my neck, his ear to my cheek. My arms slip around his back, my hands reaching under his sweater to find skin. I want to tell him I love him, but before I can, his mouth presses against my own.

TWENTY-FOUR

ANOTHER MONDAY, ANOTHER DR. MARGIE DAY.

I sit in the same wicker chair I've sat in for the past seven months and recount the events of the past week: Jasper's and my post-Thanksgiving cease-fire and the subsequent Battery Park debacle; the double shift at the Skillet and the Gilberts' Christmas-tree crisis; Ellie's and my early-morning soul connection and the superhero transformation; and lastly, Jasper's and my second, more meaningful reunion.

Dr. Margie asks me how Jasper and I left things, and I sheepishly admit that we experienced talkus interruptus due to an overwhelming need to touch each other. I don't use those exact words, of course. Still, her lips purse, and she delivers a patented, "I see."

Dr. Margie makes her usual notations, but the scribbling doesn't bother me as much as it normally does. This is because as I speak, I'm thinking about what a colossal waste of my time and Fitzi's money it is for me to be sitting in her stupid wicker chair, and about how I'd probably get better a lot quicker if I just kept talking to Ellie and started watching more Oprah.

I'm brainstorming polite ways to tell Dr. Margie this when the oven timer goes *ding* and she pulls out her appointment book. She tells me she has a dentist's appointment this time next week and asks me if it would be okay to meet at ten instead of nine. I say no, that won't be necessary. She looks up, startled.

"I think," I say, "that I've gotten all I can out of this therapy thing. So we don't need to schedule any more visits."

"I see." She puts her pencil down. "And how long have you felt this way?"

"A while," I say, even though it's really only been a day.

"Well," she says. "It's unusual to end treatment so abruptly. I think it's best for us to meet a few more times—discuss this further."

Am I not speaking clearly, or is she determined not to hear me? "I'm confused," I say. "Isn't the point of all this to equip me with the tools with which to handle my own problems?"

"Ultimately, yes."

"Well, I think I'm ready to do that."

Dr. Margie sighs softly. "Bridget, I think it's wonderful that you feel you've made so much progress." I hate the way she says that—as if even though I *feel* I've made progress, I really haven't made any at all. She continues, "But I believe there's still a lot of work we can do together."

"Like what?"

"Like figure out why you still equate physical intimacy with love."

I feel like grabbing Dr. Margie's pencil and jamming it far up her ass. How dare she say I'm stupid enough to confuse sex with love?

"Just because Jasper and I enjoy *making love* doesn't mean that we aren't *in* love," I say.

Dr. Margie nods, a small, semipatronizing smile playing on her lips. "Maybe we can reach a compromise," she says. "How about you take next Monday off, and we'll meet the following week at our usual time? If you still feel you're ready to discontinue our sessions, we'll discuss ways of making the transition." She closes the book as if it's a done deal, even though I haven't responded. I try to mask my irritation lest she take my hostility as a sign I need more therapy. I gather my things and head for the door.

I cannot believe this. Why can't she simply be happy that I'm ready to face the world on my own? Of course, me facing the world on my own means a four-hundred-dollar-per-month profit loss for her. I wonder if it's too late to have Fitzi put a stop payment on his last check to her. Maybe then she'd let me have my mental freedom.

Finals approach; Jasper switches gears into Superstudent mode. He sets up camp in my apartment, working diligently. Trying to fulfill my role as the good girlfriend, I volunteer regular neck and back massages and host a spaghetti dinner for his P-chem study group.

Somehow we muddle through the week. Jasper looks wholly spent. After his last exam—a grueling essay-based Spanish III nightmare—we spend a record twenty-three hours on my futon. He's leaving in three days, heading to New Jersey not only for the holidays but also for the whole six weeks of winter break. He's doing a stint at his uncle's landscaping and snow-removal business.

"We'll still have weekends," he says as he combs my hair with his fingers. "I'll drive down every weekend if you want."

"Wouldn't it be easier to stay here? Find a job in Newark. You can live with me rent-free."

But it's no use. Jasper smiles, dots my face with kisses, and explains patiently for the umpteenth time why Uncle Craig would disown him if he backed out two weeks before the busy season. I do understand, I guess. I just don't like it. I don't like having to say goodbye again, especially now, when things are finally feeling good and normal, as if they might have a chance at semipermanence.

His hand caresses the side of my face. "I'll make it up to you. New Year's Eve. We'll go to some fancy black-tie restaurant, and then I'll take you dancing. Do you want to go dancing?"

"Yes," I say. "I do."

He kisses me softly on the spot on my neck shaded by earlobe. "It'll be okay," he murmurs. "You'll see."

TWENTY-FIVE

WITH ALL THE TOGETHER TIME Jasper and I try to cram in before his departure, I barely have five seconds to think about what I'm getting him for Christmas, let alone any time to actually buy stuff. When Ellie calls and wants to know if I'm up for an afternoon shopping spree, I accept immediately and send Jasper back to the dorm to pack up his things.

Three hours and forty-seven stores later, I'm still at a loss. "I hate this," I moan while combing the aisles of a Toys "R" Us.

"You're being too fussy," Ellie says. "Don't overthink things."

"Oh, that's helpful."

Ellie reaches behind me, plucks a packet of Sea Monkeys

off the shelf, and hands it to me. I say, "You've got to be joking."

"Why? They're quirky, fun, moderately priced—and everybody loves Sea Monkeys."

"First of all," I say, "eew." I shove the Sea Monkeys back on the shelf. "Second of all, the guy who invented Sea Monkeys is some crazy old fart who gives bazillions of dollars to the KKK. Not exactly Peace on Earth."

"Get out!"

"No, it's true," I say. "Aunt Dorrie sent me an article about it a couple of years ago."

"Well, then."

We press on. I never realized Christmas shopping could be so trying. Most of the people I usually buy gifts for have been in my life forever, so I don't have to worry about spending too much money or sending the wrong message. Jasper is another story entirely. Clothes seem too mom-ish, toys too babyish, and a gift certificate far too impersonal.

In the end, I drop a small fortune on a bunch of crap that I'm not thrilled with but that I think illustrates the effort I've exerted: a VHS copy of A&E's biography of Bessie Smith; a lunar calendar for the upcoming year; a kiddie chemistry set for making your own bubble gum; a sixty-minute phone card with a picture of Elvis looking like Morrissey on the front; and a miniature rubber model of an anatomically correct human heart dangling from a key chain.

I wrap these things as Katharine has taught me, in papers

of a variety of colors and designs, with impeccable bows adorning each one. Next, I take a cue from Martha Stewart and design personalized gift tags on card stock, rubber-stamping gold stars and crimson holly berries on them as borders. I've barely taped the last one down when Jasper calls, saying he'll be at my apartment in forty minutes.

After a quick shower, I race around picking up stray clothes and running my trusty Swiffer Sweeper across all visible surfaces. A stick of vanilla incense smells delicious, and strategically placed candles will set a romantic mood. I spend so much time prepping the scenery that I leave myself a whopping thirteen minutes for hair, makeup, and accessories.

I fluff my curls, which have formed so nicely postshower that I decide to leave them alone. I keep cosmetics to a bare minimum—a light sweep of mascara, a bit of blush, and a quick smear of shimmery berry-colored gloss. From my closet I grab one of my favorite all-black ensembles: form-fitting ribbed turtleneck sweater tucked into a pleated wool miniskirt, paired with thick tights and platform Mary Janes. Over my hips I fasten a thin silver chain belt, which picks up the silver in the teardrop earrings dangling from my lobes. In the mirror I see the kind of person Katharine would be proud to call her daughter.

Jasper is looking particularly dapper this evening, in wide-wale navy corduroys and a rumpled white tuxedo shirt, collar and cuffs rakishly unbuttoned. He hands me a small ivory-wrapped package. "For you," he says, with a kiss to my cheekbone. I think of the pile of presents I have for him and instantly fly into panic mode. I've done it again—gone overboard. My seemingly innocuous purchases will most certainly thrust our relationship way off balance and into a state of total flux, and worse, *It's all my fault.*

"Thank you," I say calmly, placing the box on top of a stereo speaker. "Let's do presents later, okay?"

Jasper slips behind the wheel of my car, and we shoot up 95 to a swank fondue restaurant in Talleyville Plaza. The place is a maze of high-backed mahogany booths—Privacy Central—and I feel incredibly sophisticated. A very bland, very blond waiter named Brad explains how the fondue works: Once we make our selection, a big flame will shoot out of the center of our table, heating whatever fondue concoction we decide on. Jasper takes out his fake ID and orders us a bottle of chardonnay. In a few minutes, Brad returns, opens the wine, and hands Jasper the cork. Jasper flashes me a look of mild alarm, and I wrinkle my nose, *Bewitched* style, to indicate that he should sniff it. He does, and Brad pours a teensy amount into one of the long-stemmed glasses. Again, Jasper looks to me for assistance. I nod toward the glass, and when that doesn't work, I mouth, "Taste it."

"Oh, right," Jasper says. He gulps it all down in one big swig. "It's, uh, good." Brad turns to me and rolls his eyes ever so slightly. After filling our glasses, he flits off to another booth, leaving Jasper and me free to giggle at the awkward incident.

"Real slick," I say teasingly. "If you're old enough to have a fake ID, don't you think you should learn how to use it?"

"Don't be talking trash 'bout me, woman."

"Don't give me reason to."

Brad returns and walks us through the menu. I take charge and order a traditional Swiss cheese appetizer and a Seafood Delight platter for the entrée. When I finish, I notice that Jasper's staring unabashedly at my face. It makes me self-conscious.

"Don't do that," I say.

"Do what?"

"Look at me like that."

"Like what?" He reaches across the table and pulls my hand into his. "You're cute when you're feeling flustered. I'll miss that."

"Don't say that."

"But I will."

"Yeah, but don't make it sound like we're breaking up. Like you'll never see me looking flustered again."

"Is that what I said?"

"It's not *what* you said," I inform him. "It's *how* you said it."

"Right."

This is not the only thorny exchange we share during our meal. In between offering each other cheese-soaked cubes of bread and skewered chunks of lobster meat, we exchange mild barbs. By the time we're finishing the Triple Chocolate

Fantasy dessert, it's clear that neither of us is completely comfortable with the imminent separation.

After dinner I take him to the house on Red Lion Road, the one dripping with a million Christmas lights. The family that owns the house does it all themselves every year, starting the day after Thanksgiving. Color blazes from every inch of space—the roof, the driveway, the lawn. So blindingly unavoidable that all traffic slows to a near halt. Mostly people park their cars in the breakdown lane, the line a half-mile long in each direction. It's like having a little bit of Las Vegas in suburbia.

As I pull up to the house, Jasper's eyes grow as wide as the snow tires on his truck. I watch him drink it all in: the chorus line of automated elves, the bouquets of electric poinsettias, the player piano manned by a robotic Santa that spins carol after carol. We walk the perimeter of the sloping yard, neither of us saying much.

Finally, Jasper pauses and turns toward me. "Wow," he says, looking at least ten years younger. *"Wow."*

"You like?"

"Oh, yeah."

"I was afraid you'd think it was tacky."

"Well, it is," he says. "But in the good way."

"Exactly."

I tell him how my dad used to bring me here every year the Sunday after Thanksgiving; how we'd make a special detour on our way back from Aunt Dorrie's to see what new additions the year had brought. My father, the lapsed Jew, never liked Christmas much—but he loved the lights. After the divorce Katharine always did up our trees in stiff department-store décor: tiny white lights, huge mauve satin bows, silver blown-glass ornaments shaped like stars the size of softballs. "Elegant," she would say. "Victorian." Dad and I disagreed.

"Obnoxious," he'd whisper as he hugged me goodbye. "Dog-ass ugly."

"I think," Jasper says, "that our dads would have gotten along just fine."

He pulls me into a tunnel of twinkling white lights arching over the driveway and yanks a bunch of real mistletoe from his coat pocket. Holding it over my head, he says, "Merry First Christmas, Bridget Elise," and kisses me deeply. It's such a small thing, his bringing the mistletoe, but I can't remember a more romantic moment. I press myself closer into his down jacket, let my body melt into his. "I'm so in love with you," I whisper into his ear. His arms tighten around my waist.

"Good," he says. "Maybe we'll be okay after all." We stand there, holding each other, completely oblivious to the outside world.

Morning breaks too quickly. I feel my body waking up before I'm ready to get out of bed. The muscles in my arms have stiffened, and though I try to stretch them out as quietly as possible, my wrists chink loudly. Rather, my left wrist chinks loudly, as that is the one bearing Jasper's gift: an antique charm bracelet crammed with miniature silver objects of significance to us—a saddle shoe, a crescent moon, even a tiny skillet. It may be the nicest gift anyone has ever given me.

"Hey, you," Jasper murmurs. "Time is it?"

"Not time for you to leave yet."

He smiles, gently pulls me into spoon formation. "No, really, what time?"

"Eleven."

We cuddle for a minute more before Jasper begins to get ready to go. I lie on the futon and watch as he pulls on his corduroys. "What are you thinking?" he asks.

"That it's a good thing we're not on a sitcom."

"Explain, please."

"Well," I say, sitting up, "you know how on most TV shows there's always the one couple—the *will-they, won't-they* pair—and you know eventually they'll get together, usually during sweeps week. But they're never allowed to stay together long, because happy couples make for crappy ratings. So basically, if we were one of those couples, we'd be about four episodes away from total demise."

Jasper shakes his head. "I'm sure I should be troubled by your ability to compare every aspect of human existence to movies or TV, but it's damn cute."

Like a pup who's just been dubbed "good doggie," I beam

at this bit of praise. I slink closer to the edge of the mattress and pat it gently. Jasper plops down and gives me a kiss so good I don't even mind the morning breath.

We dress and head over to his dorm to load up the truck, and then go on to the Dunkin' Donuts drive-through for coffee and crullers. "You could still come up for Christmas Eve," he says while we wait.

I shake my head. "Katharine's surgery is on the twenty-second," I say. "I'd never hear the end of it if I left town, even for a night."

"You have to meet my family sometime."

"I will," I say. "I promise."

Jasper swings back to my house to drop me off. Over the loud idle of engine, he says, *"The Nanny."*

"What?"

"Successful sitcom couples. Didn't she marry that Mr. Sheffield guy?"

"Yes," I say. "Yes, she did. But the show got canceled the very next season."

"Oh."

"Call me when you get in?"

He nods and leans over for another kiss, but before our lips connect, he abruptly pulls back. "Chandler and Monica!"

"Huh?"

"They're still together, aren't they?"

"Yeah," I say. "Yeah, they are."

He grins. "So have a little faith, will you?"

With one last scrumdiddlyumtious kiss, he's gone. I watch the rear of his truck shrink into the distance, and realize that it's okay—that *I'm* okay. Someone's leaving and I'm not falling apart. Granted, it's only been a few minutes, but I have the distinct feeling that this tranquility isn't going away. Jasper's gone, but he'll be back, and I'll be here, ready and waiting.

TWENTY-SIX

THE SUNDAY AFTER JASPER LEAVES, I call Mrs. Gilbert and tell her I'm ready to pack up Benji's room.

"Wonderful," she says. "I knew you'd come around."

Although I'm prepared to drive down to the house right away, Mrs. Gilbert tells me she thinks it's better for me to come tomorrow. "The kids will be at school," she says. "It might be less traumatic for them if you do it when they're not around."

Of course, the fact that both she and Mr. Gilbert will be at work tomorrow isn't lost on me. But I say nothing. She tells me she will leave a house key under the mat and a plate of cookies on the counter.

Seeing as I have nothing to do on a Sunday afternoon, I decide it's a good time to wrap presents. It's nice to feel productive. I grab the stack of enormous shopping bags accumulating in my half kitchen and sort the presents into piles for each intended. I'm all set to get started when I realize I can't find my scissors. A laborious hunt ensues. After digging through nearly every inch of my tiny pad, I come up empty. Well, not completely empty. Shoved between a neglected wok and some recycled disposable brownie pans, I find my trusty gray sketchbook, limp and moldy and forgotten for God knows how many months. I curl up on the futon and flip through the book's musty pages.

I've never fancied myself an artist—I've had this pad for nearly four years and it's not even half used—but ever since I was introduced to charcoal in the seventh grade, I've had an on-again, off-again jones for the stuff. It strikes me as I look through these old sketches how many of them are of Benji. Posing in his hat. Eating an apple. Even the landscapes of Battery Park feature Benji lurking somewhere in the background.

And then it hits me.

Not once have I ever tried to draw myself.

I set up in front of the full-length mirror bolted to the bathroom door and begin to examine my face. It's not a bad face. Oval, but with a pointy chin. Mostly clear skin, a little too pale, but even-toned. Full mouth, nondescript nose.

It's the eyes that get me. I've been putting makeup on them since I was twelve, but I guess I take them for granted. Now I see how odd they are. A little too large for my head, and framed by lashes so long they look fake. The flesh between my lids and brows curves down a bit at the corners, creating a deep shadow on the ends closer to my nose. And the color—my driver's license lists it as brown, but it's a mottled brown, like sand and toffee and chocolate all mixed up.

As much as I try to draw them, as hard as I try to render them on the page, I can't make them look like mine. I become possessed, tearing through sheet after sheet. Trying to capture the depth, the shadows and light. I draw my eyes bigger and bigger, filling up more and more of the space, dwarfing my other features until I look like one of those Japanimation girls. I strip away the skin, drawing my head as a skull but with my eyes rolling in the sockets. I go at it until my hands are covered with sepia smudges, until my fingers are sore from grasping the russet-colored charcoal so tightly.

It's well past dinnertime when my doorbell rings unexpectedly. Ellie. "What's on your hands?" she asks, wandering into my apartment.

"Charcoal," I say. I show her the sketches.

"They're good," she says. "These last ones are kind of freaky, though. What are you trying to do?"

"See myself," I say.

"Finally," she says, and flops onto the futon.

I arrive at the Gilberts' just past nine, when I'm sure everyone has cleared out for the day. The key is under the Santa Claus welcome mat, as promised, and there is an enormous platter of oatmeal-raisin cookies on the kitchen counter, also as promised. I grab two, pour myself a glass of milk, take a deep breath, and descend into the basement.

I start with the pressboard wardrobe. Since Benji was never much of a pack rat, it's fairly empty—just a few battered board games and some clothes he'd outgrown. I set aside the navy blue suit he wore at his confirmation for Charlie, thinking he might want to wear it at his own. Pretty soon I'm making piles for everybody. To Anna I bequeath his old trench coat; to Mr. Gilbert, his childhood fencing foil and mask. I even make a stack of Benji's old records and tapes, thinking I'll send them to Jack.

It takes me about three hours to sort through the paltry contents of the room. Mostly because I find myself reminiscing over battered Superman comic books and G.I. Joe dolls missing limbs. It pains me, but I eventually place these on the piles of things that will either go to the Goodwill or into the garbage. I spend twenty minutes fingering the pocket watch. In the end, I set it in the pile intended for me.

I decide I need a lunch break before I delve into the hard stuff—the untouched trunk and boxes shipped back from California. Upstairs I whip together a mash of tuna, relish, and mayo, then spread it over a toasted bagel. I eat slowly, trying to delay the inevitable, but I get restless, so I head back down.

The trunk looks scarier than the boxes, so I skip that and rip into a carton packed tight with clothes. Those I can deal with. Socks and underwear go into the trash pile. Jeans and such go into the Goodwill heap, but only after I check all the pockets. I only find loose change and Chap Sticks, but it makes me feel better than not looking at all. T-shirts and sweaters are a little trickier. The ones I recognize from his pre-Humboldt days get divvied up between Charlie and Anna. I claim his favorite Haley sweatshirt, worn and washed so many times that the school's logo is barely discernible.

Carton number two is piled with more innocuous material—a lot of linens on top, textbooks on the bottom. I flip through the pages of each book, and there, in the middle of his Intro to Oceanography text, I find a half-written letter to Anna. I want to read it but slip it into the pocket of the trench coat instead.

It's nearing two before I'm ready to attack the trunk. Anna and Charlie will be home from school in a little over an hour, and if I leave now, I won't have to face them. But if I leave now, I'll only have to put myself through this again. I opt to stay, finishing the job in one last push.

Though Benji's things were packed meticulously, with a definite order, I don't give much thought to who packed them until I pop open the lid of the trunk. Lying on top are dozens and dozens of unopened cards and letters. I'm confused until I realize they're addressed to Benji's family, not him. Condolences from the people in his California life. It strikes me that they've just been sitting here all these months, unread, their sentiments trapped in a weird time warp. I gather them into one tall stack, wrap them in a rubber band, and set them aside.

It only gets harder.

Each layer of the trunk reveals more and more personal items. I find two shoe boxes. One lid has my name scribbled on it in Magic Marker, the other one reads *et al.* Inside rests all the correspondence and bits of care packages we all sent to him while he was away. I am shocked to find my own handwriting staring up at me. I quickly flip through the envelopes from the *et al* box, and I'm surprised to find more than two dozen letters from Ellie. Carefully, I deal the letters into mini stacks according to author, thinking each person may want them back. I decide not to comb through the *Bridget* box until I get home.

I'm infinitely relieved when I reach the ivy-covered paper lining the bottom of the trunk. All that's left are a couple of Kmart envelopes stuffed with photographs, which I don't even attempt to look through. I deposit them on top of the *Mrs. Gilbert* pile and figure she'll have to take care of them herself.

Thinking I'm finished, I go to close the lid of the trunk when I hear something thud inside. Upon further inspection, I discover a zip pouch hidden by the fabric forming the underbelly of the lid. Inside I find a small leather-bound book. How could I have not known he kept a journal?

There are three things I can do with this journal: trash it (protecting his privacy), give it to his mom (relinquishing responsibility for it), or take it home (allowing me to soak up its contents). Before I can make a rational decision, I hear the basement door creak open.

"Bridget—is that you?" Anna calls down.

"Yeah," I say. "Be up in a second."

Without further thought, I shove the journal into the *Bridget* box and charge up the stairs.

My hands shake as I pull out of the Gilberts' neighborhood. I light a cigarette, hoping to steady them, but it's not much help. As if on automatic pilot, I steer my car toward Old New Castle and park at the Battery Park wharf.

There is literally no one around, probably because it's about forty degrees outside. Still, I zip up my jacket, pull on my cherry-colored stretch mittens, and head out, Benji's leather book in my pocket. I walk quickly, eyes glued to the ground in front of me, trying to disappear into the landscape. I feel as if I'm about to do something very, very wrong, but I am either unable or unwilling to stop my actions. I grab a seat on the van Gogh bench.

The brown leather of the book's cover is smooth, almost virginal. I draw it up to my nose, breathe in its faint scent of cedar, most likely from the trunk. Inside the cover, on the first creamy page, is Benji's full name, Benjamin Kirkwood Gilbert, written in loopy script. I turn the page to the first entry, penned in the distinctively unpretentious chicken scratch I'd recognize anywhere:

> 12 June
> Got my H.S. diploma today. 3 mos. to Cali. Went
> camping @ Lums with the gang. Had an okay time.

And that's all he's written about that night. No mention of our moonlit conversation or subsequent make-out session. The pages of my own journal are covered with reflections on the incident—on the stars I saw when we kissed and how I felt every time he touched me, even in the most innocent way.

The entries that follow are eerily similar, stoic shorthand outlining mundane events, with scant explorations of their significance. The most emotion he manages to pack in doesn't pop up until the summer's half over: *Ticket to Arcata arrived in mail. Six weeks until I leave this shit hole. Can't hardly wait.*

More surprising than this paucity of passion is the glaring omission of even my name. Hadn't we known each other forever? If an archaeologist discovered this journal hundreds of years from now, he would believe that this Benjamin Kirkwood Gilbert had no one in his life: no family, no friends, and certainly no girlfriend. Jack makes a total of three appearances, usually in passing reference. Anna gets the distinction of an entire paragraph devoted to her thirteenth birthday, but it looks as if the honor had more to do with the poison oak she developed on the right side of her face than the birthday itself. I don't even surface until the day of his exodus: *B drove me to airport. Didn't cry. Flight good; got a window seat + extra snack mix. Couldn't fall asleep. Jet lag bites the big one.*

Once in California, Benji's journal seems to have morphed into an all-purpose notebook. There are lists of things to do, phone numbers of people who I assume are classmates, strange scribblings about fish and aquatic plant life. I tear through these pages, looking for my name, but I'm almost entirely absent from his life, or at least the life reflected by this diary. Finally, I do find one undated entry between homework assignments: *B left 3 messages. Didn't call back. Couldn't.* There isn't enough context for me to figure out whether the *couldn't* is a physical impossibility or an emotional one.

Impatiently, I flip to the last entry, which was written just a few days before my eighteenth birthday, roughly two weeks before his accident. It consists of four short sentences about a field trip to some oceanic reservation, followed by *Get B card?* And underneath that, in a different colored ink, the word *YES* circled three times.

I remember that card, the front of which depicted a black squirrel chewing on a pencil. Hallmark had left the inside blank, and Benji filled the space with his cramped handwriting. The letter itself wasn't anything too terribly special—just his observations about the hippie town where his school was located. What I remember most about the card—sent six weeks *after* the breakup memo—is the last paragraph. In it he said that he had been thinking about New Year's Eve, which we'd ended up spending together, and how he was glad that we had only kissed that night and not made love again, because sex would've messed everything up. *I know you don't get it,* he wrote, *but I feel myself changing into the man I want to be—and I need to find myself by myself.* He signed it, *Miss you,* followed by his name.

At the time, the card threw me into a complete tailspin. He was right; I didn't get it. If he missed me enough to say so in a card, then why wasn't I supposed to call him? Why couldn't I visit? He didn't even like the idea of my e-mailing him, and on the few occasions I did, he refused to answer.

It suddenly occurs to me that not once in ninety-odd pages has he referred to our night on the laundry pile. Not a single hint that during the time he was keeping this journal he had had any sexual activity, let alone lost his virginity. Granted, most guys don't wax poetic about doing the deed, but come on—there's not even an *Oh, yeah—finally scored.*

I start to comb the pages I've skipped when I land on a strange entry dated the week before I received the memo:

> *9 Dec.*
> *Ellie called. Said I need to break it off with B. She's*
> *right, not fair to her. Must take care of this B4 Xmas*
> *break.*

I am in complete shock. The words swim before my eyes as I read them over and over and over again. I rapidly try to form as many interpretations as possible, but they all translate to the same thing: Not only did Ellie know that Benji wanted to break up with me, but she told him to do it, and she told him to do it because it wasn't fair to her.

The fog lifts from my brain—I can suddenly view the situation with perfect clarity. The breakup memo. The twenty-six letters from Ellie in Benji's trunk. The only way his not breaking up could be unfair to her is if the two of them had been brewing something all along.

I run back to the Coach, pop the trunk. Pull out the stack of Ellie letters. Stand there reading each one, trying to figure out exactly what was said between them. Nothing significant leaps out at me at first. Finally I find an envelope postmarked early December of last year. On page three of the blue-and-white Hello Kitty stationery I find something that makes me feel sick:

> *re: bridget. you* have *to tell her. better she hear it*
> *from you than me. we can't keep going around in*
> *these circles. i can't handle the guilt, you know? she's*
> *my best friend, and i feel like i'm betraying her. don't*
> *you?*

Tears pour from my eyes. It makes perfect sense; it makes no sense at all. I never thought myself capable of so fierce an anger. I slam the trunk, throw my body into the driver's seat, and peel off in search of Ellie.

TWENTY-SEVEN

THERE IS THE USUAL AMOUNT OF DINNERTIME FUSS and flurry when I arrive at the Food-n-Stuff. Ellie is in the manager's booth, doling out lotto tickets and cigarettes to snappish customers carting screaming brats on their hips. I push my way past a particularly churlish-looking bald man trying to cash his wife's Social Security check. "I need to talk to you," I tell Ellie. *"Now."*

She clocks out and descends from the booth, her white-blond hair sprouting from her scalp in tufts trapped between shiny dragonfly hair clips. "You okay?" she asks.

"Outside," I say.

Ellie fishes a rumpled pack of cigs from her smock. "Want one?"

I shake my head.

"You don't look so good," she says.

"I don't feel so good."

She takes a few drags, fanning the smoke from her face with her hand. "So are you gonna tell me what's wrong, or are we just gonna stand here?"

I get right to the point: "Were you in love with him?"

"Who?"

"Benji."

"What? Of course not."

"Then why were you screwing around with him?"

She shakes her head, as if to clear some cobwebs from her brain. "What are you talking about?"

I pull a fistful of envelopes from my coat pocket. "Twenty-six letters in five and a half months—you do the math."

"Where did you get those?"

"You have to tell her," I read. *"Better she hear it from you than me."*

She blanches. "Oh my God," she says. "It's not what you think."

"What I think," I say, "is that you were trying to steal my boyfriend."

Her cigarette drops to the sidewalk, and she stomps on it with her hot-pink clogs. "You should know me better than that."

"I thought I did."

"I didn't know how to tell you," she says. "And after a while, it didn't seem that important. But Benji—he used to call me sometimes. To talk about you. About . . . things."

"What things?"

"You know—*stuff*. Thoughts. Feelings." She looks toward one of the bag boys corralling carts in the parking lot. "Doubts. But we weren't having some sordid affair." She shakes out another cigarette, lights it up. "Are you sure you don't want one?" When I don't answer, she continues, "It was never about him wanting someone else, you know. He just—he wasn't sure if he wanted *you*."

Her words hit me harder than any admission of guilt ever could, because I know they hold some semblance of truth. "You're lying," I splutter.

"Bridget—no."

"Even if you're not, why didn't you tell me? You were my friend first."

"I didn't want to hurt you."

"And you think it doesn't, me finding out like this?" Once again, I'm crying in a public place. I wipe snot from my nose. "How long did you know? Huh? How could you? Let me walk around like some kind of stupid . . ." Ellie reaches for my arm, and I instantly recoil. "Don't touch me," I snarl.

I throw the crumpled letters at her face. They scatter like snowflakes. "I hope he was worth it."

I make my exit with as much dignity as I can possibly muster. For the record, it isn't much.

Later that night, I call Jasper and tell him about my day. Even as I speak, I'm wondering if it's the right thing to

179

do—if he's the right person to confide in. But at this moment, he's all I have. My face contracts, preparing for more tears, but none come. I'm all cried out.

"I'm sorry, honey," Jasper says, his voice oozing comfort. "It must've been hard for you."

There's a long pause. I hear the TV in the background. Is he even paying attention to me?

"That's it?" I say. "That's all you have to say?"

"Um, why don't you tell me what you want to hear, and then I'll go ahead and say that."

"You're not funny."

"I wasn't trying to be."

In a situation like this, my ideal boyfriend would want so badly to comfort me, no distance could keep him from my doorstep. He'd hitchhike if he had to, just so he could put his arms around me, make me believe that everything was going to be okay.

"Mom's got dinner on the table," Jasper says. "Call you tomorrow?"

My ideal boyfriend would *not* be trying to end our current conversation. "But I need you *now*."

He sighs. "Look, I haven't eaten since breakfast. Give me twenty minutes, okay?"

"Forget it," I say. "Don't call at all."

I hang the phone up hard, without another word, fully expecting him to call back immediately. He doesn't. Twenty minutes go by. An hour. He's not calling back. Doesn't he know that a hang-up is girl-speak for "Call me back and find out what's wrong"? Maybe he does and doesn't care.

Against my better judgment, I call him. "I can't believe you didn't call me back."

"You hung up on me."

"Exactly."

He says, "I don't know what you want from me," to which I respond, "I want you to make it better."

"How?" he asks. "How can *I* make it better? I'm not *him,* Bridget. I'm not Benji."

"I know that," I snap.

"Do you?"

"You don't get it," I say. "You never will." With that, I hang up again. The phone rings less than a minute later, but I don't answer it, and he doesn't leave a message. Rather than deal with the implications of these actions, I pop a Xanax and slink into my bed.

TWENTY-EIGHT

A WEIRD BUZZING ROUSES ME AROUND ONE A.M.; it takes me a few minutes to realize it's the doorbell. I scurry downstairs, thinking in my bleary, half-awake state that it's Jasper. But when I call his name, no one answers. I grab an empty wine bottle from the recycling bin for protection and open the door wide enough for a wedge of light to creep through.

"Hey, you."

It's Jack Doyle. Standing on my doorstep. At one o'clock in the morning.

I rub some of the sleep from my eyes. "What are you doing here?"

"I know it's late—sorry."

"Do you want to come in?" I ask. Jack shakes his head. "Do you want me to come out?" He nods. I sigh. "Give me a second."

Jack stays on the stoop as I duck back in to grab a pair of sneakers and a coat. When I emerge, he points to his car and says, "C'mon."

"Where are we going?" I ask. He doesn't answer. I get in anyway.

Jack pulls away from the curb before I've clicked my seat belt in place. The inside of the car smells like root beer and cinnamon gum. I try again. "Where are we going?"

"Not far," he says. "Relax."

In a few minutes, we've reached our destination: Raymond Stadium, the westernmost point of campus. Jack kills the lights as he turns into the parking lot, slips the car into a dark spot under a massive oak tree. "We're here."

We get out of the car and walk halfway around the building to a heavy chain-link fence by the back bleachers. "Hold this," Jack says, handing me a six-pack. He then proceeds to scale the fence with the strength and agility of Spider-Man, landing gracefully on the other side. "Your turn."

"I can't climb this thing," I say.

"Sure you can."

"Jack . . ."

"Gimme that," he says, reaching over for the beer.

I sigh heavily, grab the top of the fence with my hands, and stick the tip of my sneaker into an opening. Hoisting myself upward, I swing my right leg over so that essentially I'm left straddling the thin, cold metal.

"Now what?"

Jack surveys the situation. "Twist left, bring your other leg over, and drop. There—you got it."

My feet hit the ground with a less-than-delicate thump. I smooth the T-shirt beneath my coat and glare at Jack. "Why are we here?"

He presses a finger to his lips. "Shhh." My body springs to attention, thinking he's heard something, but Jack simply takes my hand in his and leads me to the field.

When we hit the fifty-yard line, Jack wriggles out of his black leather jacket and lays it on the grass. He tells me to sit, motioning to the jacket, and I do. After tossing me a can of beer, he plunks down next to me and cracks one open for himself.

"So how are you?" he asks. He shakes some foam from his hand.

"Okay," I say. "You?"

"Not bad." He eyes my unopened beer. "You *are* going to drink that, aren't you?" He punctuates this question with an extra-long gulp, followed by a deep, thunderous belch, and chases it with a shit-eating grin.

I open the can, take a tentative sip. It tastes like crap, but Jack looks on approvingly, and I drink a little harder, waiting for the warmth to creep into my cheeks.

"So how's Boston?" I say, mostly to fill the void.

"Good, good. Berklee—I thought I knew jazz, you know, growing up with it, but you can't really *know* it until you live it, you know?"

I nod as if I understand. "What about Echo? How's she doing?"

Jack's eyes scrunch slightly. "I don't know. We broke up a while ago."

"You're kidding. When?"

"A couple of months after . . ." His voice trails off, but I can fill in the rest: a couple of months after Benji died. And so there it is, the unspoken subject, looming over us like the goalposts we're situated between.

"Look, Jack—"

"You want to know why I brought you here. I know." He pauses dramatically, sucks in a breath, lets it out slowly. "So here's the thing: We were the only ones who really knew him, who got what he was all about. But we never talked about him, never talked about what happened."

"What happened is he died. End of story."

"It's not, and you know it."

"It is for me."

Jack sighs and works on his beer. A light breeze musses the front of his caramel-colored hair. In profile, he looks remarkably like our dead friend—same WASPy nose, bow-shaped upper lip, and strong chin. But there's a hardness to Jack's face, a certain raw-boned look that never quite manifested itself on Benji's. His hair is darker than Benji's was, his skin more pink than golden, but they still could've passed for brothers, or at least first cousins.

"We used to come here, me and Benji," he says. "Mostly

in the summer, after a Denny's run. Something about this field. Marched here a few times, with the All-State band. Great field."

"I can see you're in the mood to stroll down memory lane," I say, "but I've had a shitty day, I'm really cold, and I'd like to go home."

"Why?"

"I just told you—I'm cold and I'm crabby."

"No," he says. "I meant, why was your day so shitty?"

"Long story."

"I have a few minutes."

And this is how I come to tell Jack things that, were I in a more alert frame of mind, I'd never dream of telling him. About the creepy Gilberts, and finding all those letters, and realizing that my best girlfriend was trying to snatch my boyfriend away from me. To my great relief, he expresses shock and disgust at all the appropriate moments, and offers me comfort in the form of reassuring hand squeezes and subsequent beers.

"You don't think they were—*you know*—do you?"

"I don't know what to think," I say. "Did he ever say anything to you?"

"About Ellie, or about you?"

"Well, Ellie," I answer. "Why, did he tell you stuff about me?"

"First of all, no to the Ellie question. If they wuz bumpin' uglies, I didn't know nuthin' about it. And second of all, of course Ben and I talked about you—just not in that way."

186

I guess I look skeptical, because Jack continues, "Let me try this again. Me and Benji—we were friends since first grade. And then five years later, you wandered along, and that was that. We were it for him. His buddy and his girl."

"But I wasn't," I say. "I wasn't his girl. Not for years and years."

Jack looks at me as if I've just descended Mount Sinai with a head full of recently grayed hair. "Bridget—you *have* to know how he felt about you."

"According to Ellie, he was full of doubts."

"Ah, what does she know." Jack tosses me the last can of beer. I chew over his words as I crack it open. The beer, still cold, sends a fireball into my stomach.

Jack's craggy voice interrupts my thoughts. "What does it matter, anyway? You know?"

"No," I say. "I don't."

He tucks his knees up under his chin, pensive. "You can't rewrite the past. Nothing Ellie says can really change what you had with him."

"That's just it," I say. "I don't know what we had."

He raps his knuckles against my scalp. "Um, hello? You loved him—fact indisputable."

"So?" I say. "He didn't. He didn't love me, Jack. Despite what you may think. He *told* me that. He said, 'I've tried to love you as much as you love me but the truth is I don't.' *That's* indisputable."

We're quiet for a while, both of us trying to ingest what's

been said. Or at least I am. After all, a dead Benji who didn't love me is very different from one who maybe did.

The hard crunch of beer can against semifrozen ground startles me back to attention. "I think you're wrong, Bridge," Jack says. "I mean, what really matters is that *you* loved *him*. You loved him, Bridget. Don't you see the beauty in that? Not everybody can love like that. I know I never have."

The warmth of the beer in my belly spreads up to the tips of my ears, or maybe it's Jack's long fingers twining through my hair. "Not even Echo?" I ask softly.

"No," he says. "Not even her."

Jack's lips startle mine in a kiss so unexpected I can't help returning it. It's a good kiss—soft, but not wimpy; moist, but not sloppy. The pressure of his face against mine makes me lean backward until I'm splayed on the field, Jack's chest covering my own. His hands cradle my face, his knee pries open the space between my legs. Logically, I know this is wrong, but I have separated from my body. I hover over the two of us, watching with detached curiosity as Jack's tongue draws Celtic knots on my neck and my hands fumble with the button on his jeans.

And then there's a loud crash—two cars slamming into each other on the nearby road. The noise jerks us both back into our bodies. "Stop," I say, but Jack rolls off me before I've finished asking him to. I bolt upright, smoothing my tousled hair. "I have a boyfriend," I say, experiencing a sharp pang of déjà vu.

Jack nods, as if he already knows. Wordlessly, we gather

the empty cans and head back to the fence. Once we're safe on the other side, we see the accident—a navy blue SUV up against the accordion-pleated bumper of some little crap car the color of the Brady Bunch's kitchen. I don't want to look at it. I don't want to think about the people inside, about the ways their lives will be altered by this moment. No one is moving. It's dark, and there is no one on the street, except for us.

Jack sprints over to the SUV, and I follow him, shaking. A guy shouts at us from the gas station across the street, saying he's already called 911. In the distance we hear the wail of a siren. Two cop cars and an ambulance arrive on the scene. Jack talks to one of the officers. In the dim streetlight I can see him pointing at me. It feels like hours before he leaves the cop's side.

"Let's go," he says finally. "Let's get you out of here."

I'm practically catatonic by the time Jack pulls up in front of my house. "You okay?" he asks.

"Yeah," I lie.

"I'm sorry for—you know."

"It's okay." Another lie.

"I'm glad we talked, though," he says. "We should do it more often."

I say, "I'd like that," even though I don't think I would, and we hug goodbye. I watch him drive away, my head muddled, thinking, *What does it all mean?* All the while knowing that I can't figure it out in one night, or even one year.

TWENTY-NINE

I PARK IN THE VISITORS' LOT OF ST. FRANCIS HOSPITAL, feeling queasy before I even enter the building. I've never liked hospitals. They smell like death. Antiseptic death.

Fitzi is waiting for me in the gift shop. "Hey, kiddo," he says wearily.

"How's she doing?"

"Good, good," he says. "Everything according to plan. No complications. They're moving her out of recovery as we speak." He fingers a display of limping Mylar balloons greatly in need of a helium refill. "What do you think? Think she'd like these?"

"I think you better stick to roses," I say, slipping my arms around his waist. We hug awkwardly in the cramped store. "You holding up okay, Fitz?"

"Yeah, thanks," he says. "But I'll feel a lot better once I can see her."

The Katharine that awaits us in Room 307 isn't the one we're expecting. This Katharine is beyond pale, her thin skin giving off a grayish cast. I steal a look at her—eyes swollen, hair frizzed from perspiration, lips the color of uncooked liver, puffed and parted loosely—and fight the urge to flee the room. How can someone being worked on from the waist down look so damaged from the neck up?

"How ya doing, doll?" Fitzi croons as he leans over Katharine's shell of a body, planting light kisses on her cheek.

"Honey," she says, her speech thick and blurred, as if she has a sock stuck in the back of her throat. Her naked eyes widen as they catch sight of me. "What are you doing here?"

Fitzi tosses me a helpless look. I take a deep breath, sit on the edge of Katharine's bed. "I'm here," I say brightly, "because you forgot to tell me what you wanted for Christmas."

She smiles weakly. "How about a new uterus?"

This sad attempt at humor hits me like an elephant tranquilizer, but the sound of Fitzi's robust laughter snaps me to attention. "That's a good one, doll," he says. "Real good." His thick fingers stroke Katharine's delicate, blue-veined hand.

We make awkward chitchat for the next few minutes,

until a brisk nurse bustles in and tells us Katharine needs her rest. "Two hours," she says crisply. "You can come back then." Grateful, I practically run from the peach-walled room, grab a spot of floor down the hall, and promptly burst into silent tears.

As I sob into my hands, I feel the tickle of cloth against my wrists. Fitzi's handkerchief. "Thanks," I say, blowing my drippy nose. "Guess you don't want this back, huh?"

"Keep it."

To my surprise, Fitzi drops to the floor next to me. Both of us have our legs sticking straight out, though his reach about ten inches past mine. Our feet lean toward each other—if we were the same height, our shoes would be kissing. Fitzi sets his arm around my shoulder and pulls me to him, rocking me gently as I sniffle up more tears.

The nurse returns, giving us a comically stern lecture about why we can't congregate on the hospital's floor. "There's a cafeteria downstairs," she says. "Why don't you two rest there?"

We trek down; Fitzi deposits me at a plastic table and picks us up a couple of mugs of sludge coffee and a sandwich he says is tuna salad on rye, though it looks so much like cat food that neither of us is brave enough to take a nibble.

"I don't know why I'm so upset," I say, pouring a fifth packet of sugar into my caffeinated mud. "It's not like she has cancer. It's not like she's *dying*."

I can't believe I just said that.

"Fitzi—"

"No, no," he says. "You're right. She's *not* dying. She's gonna be with us for a long time, your mom. I thank God for that every day." He crosses himself fervently.

I want to ask him about his first wife, about losing her at such a young age, but we don't talk about Joyce. We never have. Most of what I know about her comes from fragmented conversations with Katharine. But I've never broached the subject with him directly, and, out of the same respect, he never tries to talk about Benji in specifics. I guess it's our way of letting the dead rest in peace.

"How are *you* holding up, kiddo?" Fitzi asks suddenly.

"With this or in general?"

"Both."

I shake my head. "Not so good, Fitz."

"I figured," he says. "The first year's the hardest. Especially around the holidays. Took me three years before I stopped buying Joyce presents."

"Really?"

"Oh yeah," he says. "Bought her presents, wrote her letters, made sure not to sleep on her side of the bed. She loved grapefruit—we always had some in the house—and I kept stocking it, even though I never ate the stuff. Would've felt strange, not having it in the fridge."

I tell him about my notebook of letters to Benji, the ones I write at the park. I tell him about the shrine, and the macabre pictures in my sketchbook, and the cache of mementos I keep in the fireproof lockbox at the bottom of my closet.

And then I tell him about Jasper, and about how good he is to me, and how happy he makes me. I show him the charm bracelet on my wrist and tell him the stories behind each trinket. But then I remember what happened last night—our long-distance argument and my accidental transgression with Jack—and it's as if I can feel all the joy being sucked from my body.

"I screwed up," I say. "It's not the first time, either."

He tries to comfort me, but I'll have none of that.

I say, "You don't understand. I did a bad thing, and I don't even know why I did it. It's just . . . I try so hard to hold it all together. But it's no good. I don't know what I'm doing. And I'm so . . . *angry* . . . all the time. At Ellie and the Gilberts and Katharine and my dad—Where is *he*? Why doesn't he call or write?"

Fitzi's handkerchief grows moist and limp in my hands. I realize I'm blubbering incoherently, but I can't seem to stop. The strangest thing is, no one around us seems to notice, or if they do, they don't seem to care. We are, after all, in the cafeteria of a hospital.

"I've been thinking," Fitzi says after I get myself under control. "I know you're not gonna like this, but I think you should come home. Not just for Christmas, but until you start school in February. And I think you should quit your job, too. You never took any time off, not for yourself, and it can't be good for you."

"Okay," I say, surprising myself at how easily I agree.

"Don't fight me on this, Bridget. I'm only looking out for your best interests."

"I said okay."

He looks more puzzled than shocked. "Really?"

"Yeah," I say. "I think I'd like that."

"Good, good," he says, beaming. "It'll be nice, all three of us under one roof again, huh?"

"I don't know about nice," I say, "but it'll definitely be interesting."

THIRTY

CHRISTMAS COMES AND CHRISTMAS GOES—it's neither terrible nor memorable, save for Katharine's inability to run the show independently. She spends much of her time on the dark red velvet settee in the living room, staring at the tree and pointing out "glaring" imperfections in its decoration, which she herself completed before surgery. She constantly rings the antique pearl-handled bell Fitzi gave her to summon assistance. Usually she only wants one of us to move a blown-glass angel ornament from one side of the tree to the other.

Fitzi, God love him, transforms into the Dork of Christmas Present, donning a tacky reindeer-embroidered sweater and fur-trimmed Santa hat. To boost our family bonding, he has banished all visitors from our house and declined all invitations to theirs. Our mostly sequestered existence is scored by an endless concert of chirpy Christmas CDs, including a classic Carpenters album more cloying than the fruitcake Fitzi's eighty-year-old aunt Estelle sends us each year.

I have been on my best behavior, partly because it means so much to Fitzi and partly because I'm hoping for a little karmic reprieve. Though I've spoken to Jasper every night since he left Newark, I still haven't been able to fess up about my night with Jack Doyle. I haven't been able to face the Gilberts, either. I conveniently dropped off their presents on Christmas Eve, when I knew they'd be at their church's vigil. And Ellie's presents, not yet wrapped, are gathered in a Target bag at my apartment. I can't bring myself to return them, not yet anyway, but I'm in no hurry to speak with their intended. Apparently she feels the same.

In a sane world, the brilliant façade I've constructed would be on the verge of collapsing. But in my world, I appear calm, cool, and even collected. Somehow I am keeping it together. Perhaps this is the result of the dozens of lies I tell myself by the hour. Like that being here with Fitzi and Katharine is something I want rather than something I need. Or that even though I am currently jobless and using parental funding to make rent, I am not sacrificing my hard-earned independence and reverting to the girl I once was. Or that if I am indeed reverting, that too is okay, because my father's abandonment forced me to grow up too quickly and I am owed a chance at carefree kid-dom.

But the weary truth is that I will never lead a carefree life, and no self-generated lie can mask this. I am, as Dr. Margie reminds me in the sessions I begrudgingly continue to attend, a sum of all parts. What she doesn't recognize is that my parts are all twisted and tarnished, and though I try to rearrange them into something I can feel proud of, I can't get there from here.

And yet there is a tiny seedling of hope rooted so deep inside me that I'm almost convinced the new year will bring a new me. There are certain quirky superstitions I've formed throughout my life, like kissing my hand and slapping it against the roof of my car as I drive through a yellow light to keep it from turning red, or eating the entire fortune cookie before reading my fortune to make sure it comes true. But the one I've felt most strongly about is the power of New Year's Eve, the belief that who you spend that evening with and how you spend it portend with whom and how you will spend the rest of that year.

Of course, I did spend last New Year's Eve with Benji, and we all know how *that* turned out.

He wasn't supposed to be at the party, but his other options consisted of attending a prayer vigil with his parents or staying home alone. I think Jack talked him into it in the end, because the four of us—Jack and Echo, Benji and me—drove together to Ellie's. Her parents had gone on a booze cruise in Philly, and as soon as she found out the house would be free, Ellie wasted no time in planning the kind of wild party you think exists only in the teen-movie universe.

There was a deejay scratching the *Brady Bunch* theme into Joni Mitchell dance remixes. Two girls in sparkly miniskirts and baby T-shirts glittered as they danced under the disco ball and strobe lights Ellie's cousin Bruno had rigged up. Echo had contributed bucket after bucket of dry ice, illegally obtained from the theatrical effects store her dad managed in Dover.

I'd never been much of a party girl, probably because Benji was never much of a party boy, and it wasn't long before the two of us escaped to the bathroom adjoining Ellie's parents' bedroom. Benji combed through the medicine chest, looking for a cure for the headache the party's throbbing music had induced, while I sipped the red plastic cup of strawberry Boone's Ellie had poured for me when we arrived two hours earlier. I was wearing a clingy dress of some shimmery pewter-colored material that rustled every time I moved. But it maximized my boobs and minimized my hips, and even Benji had to admit I looked fabulous.

He sat on the edge of the powder blue tub and said, "How'd we get here?"

"Literally or metaphorically?"

"What do you think?"

I dumped the contents of my cup into the sink. "I don't know," I said. "But I think I was happier before."

He said, "Before when?"

"I don't know," I said. "Just before."

Benji nodded. "I know what you mean."

Outside the door, we heard someone retching. Benji rolled his eyes and I laughed nervously. It was the most time we'd spent alone since he'd come back from California.

Suddenly, and seemingly out of nowhere, Benji asked me to dance.

"What, here? In the bathroom?"

"Have you ever realized," he said, "that in all the years we've known each other, we've never once danced? Why is that?"

"I would have," I said. "But you never asked."

"I'm asking now."

And so we slow-danced in the cramped bathroom, abdomens pressed close, our bodies moving to a rhythm we invented in our heads. I was afraid to talk, afraid he'd change his mind, afraid these feelings would disappear. There was kissing too, so much kissing. "Let's get out of here," he whispered huskily.

So we ditched Jack and Echo, and drove back to his house, and tussled on his bed, and I thought we were about to have an encore of the laundry incident, but then Benji stopped abruptly. "I'm sorry," he said. "I'm so sorry." I assured him it was all right, and as a gesture of goodwill I took his hand and placed it on my breast.

"No," he said, pulling away. "You deserve better."

"I want *you*," I said.

"Bridget, it's not fair. I can't do this." We lay on our backs and held hands. "Besides, I'm leaving in two days," he said. "I don't know when I'll be back."

"I'll wait for you."

"But what if I never come back?"

"Then I'll come find you."

We clambered up the stairs and turned on Dick Clark just in time to watch the ball drop, and I wasn't stupid enough to expect a kiss but there it was, Benji's mouth latched on to mine, and I thought, *It's a sign.*

Six weeks later, he was dead.

THIRTY-ONE

I SQUIRT SOME MORE OF THE DARK BROWN LIQUID onto my scalp, pulling clumps of gel through the strands of my once-cinnamon-colored hair. The smell of the dye combined with that of the rubber gloves protecting my hands makes me gag. Usually I can work a bottle of dye through my hair in less than twelve minutes, but now I take my time, checking every layer, every angle, making sure every wisp is coated with the stuff.

I'm going back to my roots—literally. It's something I've thought about for a while. The whole auburn thing started when I was fourteen, as a result of Benji's commenting on the beauty of Katharine's color. I've been keeping it up out of habit more than anything else. Yesterday, Katharine noted that I was a little overdue for a touch-up, and I practically bolted for the Happy Harry's drugstore—any excuse to get out of the house. There, in the aisles, I reached for my usual bottle of Nice 'n Easy and thought, *Why?* So I took a few minutes at the display, trying to find a shade that matched my natural color. "Espresso" came close enough.

With one last squirt, I finish off the bottle and toss the applicator into the trash. Gloves still in place, I smush my hair into a plastic shopping bag, squeeze out the air, and tie the handles together at the nape of my neck. Twenty-five minutes later, I hop into the shower to rinse the gook off and emerge a full-blown brunette.

As startled as I am by the change, Katharine is even more so. "My God," she says when I've finished blowing my new hair dry. "It's uncanny."

"What is?"

"How much you look like your father."

I offer a sheepish grin. "Sorry about that."

"Don't be," she says. "He was quite handsome." She reaches up, combing through some loose curls with her fingers. "Nice," she says. "Very striking."

"Thanks."

"So where is your young man taking you this evening?"

"I don't know," I say. "He wants it to be a surprise. All he'll tell me is that I should be dressed to kill."

"You know," she says, "I have a darling champagne-colored sheath you can borrow, if you like. It would really set off that hair."

"Um, okay."

I help her up the stairs and into the master bedroom—

though the doctor says Katharine's healing at a normal rate, her range of movement is still limited. She sits on the side edge of her and Fitzi's enormous mahogany sleigh bed and shouts directions to me as I attempt to navigate her expansive walk-in closet. Katharine's anal nature has led to impeccable organization: All garments are sorted by type, fabric, and color.

The dress Katharine has offered is less darling than it is stunning: a sleeveless satin sheath with a band of matte satin around the bust, accompanied by a matching wrap. I exit the closet and hold it up for her approval.

"Yes!" she says giddily. "That's the one! Go try it on, Bridget."

I do as I am told, surprised to discover that the dress fits perfectly. I'm also shocked to feel a price tag poking my side. Not only has Katharine never worn the dress, she also paid around $1,700 for it. On *sale*.

"I can't borrow this," I say as I exit the closet for the second time. "You spent a fortune on it."

"Oh, hush," she says. "It's absolutely exquisite on you. Fetch my jewelry box, will you? I have a set of pearls that will look simply divine."

Dutifully, I bring her the large, velvet-lined chest, the one where she keeps "the good stuff." She extracts the promised pearls, a triple-strand choker that fastens with a brushed-gold hoop at the front. Next, earrings, each consisting of one enormous pearl with a sizable diamond attached to it like a parasite. I don't even want to guess how much this all cost.

"Shoes! You need shoes. Take the beige Pradas, sweetheart. The ones with the two-inch heels."

"Mom," I say. "I am *not* wearing your zillion-dollar Prada shoes. I can't handle that much responsibility. What if I scuff them or something?"

But Katharine is clearly not listening. "You called me Mom," she says.

"So?"

"So you never call me that. Always Mother, or Katharine. I can't even remember the last time you actually said Mom."

It would be so easy for me to come back at her with something like "Well, you never acted like a mom," but I don't. Instead, I say, "Are you really going to let me walk out of the house wearing thousands of dollars' worth of your finery?"

"Why not?"

"You used to scream at me when I borrowed your umbrella!"

"Bridget," she says, "don't ruin this for me. Let me enjoy the Mom bit for at least another hour."

And so, when Jasper rings the doorbell at precisely six o'clock, I greet him dressed in head-to-toe Katharine.

"Wow," he says. "You look like a movie star."

"Thanks," I say.

"Are the parents around?"

"Upstairs. I'm supposed to announce your arrival."

"Ah," he says. "So I guess it'd be okay if I do this."

He slips a hand around the back of my head and pulls me to him, giving me a high-passion kiss. It's a shame I'm too anxious to enjoy it.

"You changed your hair," he notes as I lead him into the house.

"You hate it."

"No, no—I think it's stylin'." He grins. I'm such a sucker for that grin.

"C'mon," I say. "It's time you met the fam."

I keep the introductions brief but sweet. Fitzi is his usual jovial self, and Katharine really turns on the charm. After ten minutes of light banter, I say, "We have to get going. We have reservations."

"Of course, of course," Fitzi says. "You kids have a happy new year. And Jasper—if you don't want to make the drive back to Jersey tonight, you stay here. We have plenty of room."

They shake hands; Katharine insists on giving Jasper a kiss. "It was delightful to meet you," she says. "You must come to dinner soon."

"I'd like that," Jasper says. His sincerity is almost touching.

We head out, and I'm surprised to find that Jasper's truck is nowhere in sight. Instead, there's a sleek black Saturn parked near the end of the drive. "You like?" he asks, unlocking the passenger-side door.

"You borrow this?"

"Naw," he says. "I'm buying this."

The seats are comfy enough, but it's strange not having to

climb up onto a cracked leather bench. "I can't believe you sold the truck."

"Yeah, it hurt. But it was sucking money like a fiend. This baby's brand-new. And the mileage! Out of this world."

"Jeez," I say. "You sound like a middle-aged man."

"Least I got my sexy girlfriend to keep me young."

We head into the city, to the Columbus Room. It's an old-money establishment, with gorgeous dark wood floors, a swank leather bar, a waiter whose sole job is to pass out bread, and another one who comes around a few minutes later to sweep up the crumbs. It's the kind of place Katharine aspired to in the pre-Fitzi days, when we were still poor. It's not the kind of place I'd ever expect Jasper to take me.

As we dig into our asparagus-and-brie salad/sculpture, I ask him if he's noticed that we're the only customers under thirty.

"No," he says, grinning. "I hadn't."

"Strange vibe in here."

"Hadn't noticed that either."

Something's not right. It feels forced, our being here, as if we're two kids playing at being adults. Jasper, with his sensible car and filet mignon cooked medium-well. Me, with my designer costume and lobster tail. Restaurants—we've spent half of our relationship in restaurants. The other half we've spent in bed. But we talk—don't we? We fight, we make up. Drama dotted with laughter. My specialty.

After our dinner plates have been cleared, Jasper tries to tempt me with a chocolate-raspberry soufflé, but I'm not in the mood for dessert. "This place is making me itchy," I say. "Let's get out of here."

"You feeling okay?" he asks as we wait for the valet to bring the Saturn around.

"Actually," I say, "not so much."

"It was the lobster, wasn't it? It's disagreeing with you."

"No, we got along fine."

"Is it one of those 'We need to talk' things?"

"Yes," I say. "I think so."

"Oh."

We get into the car. Jasper asks me if I have a particular destination in mind, but I don't. He shoots onto 95 South, heading, I suppose, toward Fitzi's house. After a few minutes, he says, "So what's on your mind?" He stares straight ahead, his hands on the wheel at ten and two, his back as rigid as if it were attached to a metal pole.

I take a deep breath, let it out slowly. "Remember that night I hung up on you?"

"Yeah."

"Well, later than night, Jack Doyle—Benji's friend?—he came by to see me."

"Okay."

"He wanted to talk to me about Benji, and so we did. But then the next thing I knew, he was kissing me." My muscles involuntarily contract, the way they do when I'm merging into high-speed traffic.

"He kissed you."

"Yeah."

"So?"

"So he *kissed* me. Like, a kiss-kiss."

Jasper falls behind a VW Beetle cruising at about forty. "Well, at least you didn't kiss him."

"I didn't *not* kiss him," I say. "I mean, I kissed him back."

"Did you do anything else with him?"

"No."

"So what's the big deal?"

His passiveness infuriates me. "The big deal is that I cheated on you."

"I don't know if that's cheating, exactly."

I toss my head defiantly. "Oh yeah? Tell me then—what's your definition of fidelity?"

"I don't get it, Bridge," he says slowly. "Do you *want* me to be mad at you?"

"I want you to be *something*," I say.

"Do I like that you kissed another guy? No. Is it worth getting riled up about? No."

The words sink into my skull slowly. I have to admit, he's right. In the grand scheme of our troubled relationship, my kissing Jack is not that big a deal. But therein lies the true problem. *Our troubled relationship.* There have always been three of us in it. The Bermuda Love Triangle. The unwitting *ménage à trois.* For better or for worse, usually the latter, because death did us part, and because, like Katharine, I've never been good at being alone.

"Pull over," I say.

"Where?"

"Take the next exit. I don't care."

Jasper dutifully eases the car off the highway and down the street a bit, pulling into the parking lot of a nearby strip mall.

"Why are you doing this?" he says. "Is it some biological defect in you? Some strange deficiency that makes it impossible for you to be happy?"

"Don't yell at me."

"I'm not yelling at you!" Jasper slams his hand on the steering wheel. "Fuck!"

"I'm sorry," I say.

He doesn't look at me and he doesn't answer. Blood pulses in my ears. I want to say the right words that will make him do the right things that will make me feel the right ways, but I know deep down that the space between us will only grow wider. We can try to fill it with food and sex and clever conversation, and maybe those things can mask what's wrong, but they can't fix it and they can't make it go away.

"It's over, isn't it?"

"I think," I say, "it was over before it began."

He nods, throws the car in gear. Back on the highway. Now it's my turn to look out the window. I can feel him crying even before I hear it, and his boy tears make my heart hurt. I press a fist into my chest, trying to stop the pain.

We pull up to the house. "This is it," he says. "I mean it. I can't—"

"I know," I say. "Neither can I."

Jasper wipes his nose with the back of his hand. "I can't believe this. I can't believe you're breaking up with me."

The ache in my chest throbs hard. I apologize again and open the car door. But as I start to leave, Jasper reaches for my arm. "Don't," he says. It's almost more than I can take.

I lean over to him, let my lips graze his one final time. Then, shaking, I ease out of the car, closing the door gently behind me. As I straighten the twisted hem of Katharine's satin dress, I hear the whir of a power window retracting. Jasper leans across the passenger seat and says, "You'll regret this, you know."

"Maybe," I say. "Probably."

"Fuck you," he says through a sniffle, and he drives away.

Numb, I walk around the side of the house, my feet crunching on frosted grass. I let myself in through the back door and silently climb the stairs to the room I'm staying in, the room that used to be mine when Katharine and I moved in nearly six years ago. The walls were blue then, sapphire blue, like Benji's eyes. I'd chosen the color myself, and though my mother had objected, Fitzi overruled. "Let the kid have what she wants," he said. And so I got my blue walls, and I covered them with posters of musicians I no longer listen to and pictures of people I no longer know. And it was my room, I owned it, I made it mine.

The summer before my senior year in high school, I spent a week in Chicago visiting my aunt Dorrie and the cousins. In my absence, Katharine took it upon herself to redo "my" room. She hired a team of painters to bury the blue walls under layers of matte eggshell. ("Four coats," she told me later. "Took four coats to get rid of that ghastly blue.") She stripped the bed of my black-and-white-striped sheets, tossed away the sparkly silver curtains Ellie had stitched for me from a bolt of fabric we found at the Salvation Army. She peeled off the silk cabbage roses I'd hot-glued to the windowpanes, moved my Eiffel Tower floor lamp to the damp cellar, and gave my white shag throw rug to the paperboy.

She obliterated all traces of me, replacing the rest of my "junk" with antiques and fine fabrics in muted tones of jade. And yet she continued to call it my room. "Doesn't your room look fabulous?" she asked when I returned and was shown the final results. If she'd done it the year before, I would've fought back. I would've raised hell. But at that point, I was through fighting. In less than nine months, I would be graduating, getting out from under her thumb, becoming my own person. "Fabulous," I said dully. Anything to shut her up.

And so I stand here, dressed in borrowed clothes, in a room that's not mine. I pluck her pearls from my ears, unclasp the ones around my neck, and place them on the top of a gleaming chest of drawers. Slowly, I peel the satin from my skin, letting it fall to the polished oak floor. I unhook my strapless bra, slip off my stockings, step out of my panties. Stare at my nakedness in the large gilt-framed mirror hanging over the chest.

This is what's mine. My body. My neck, my arms, my knees. *Mine*.

It strikes me that until this very moment, I've lived my life as a reflection of other people. I've made choices because they were the opposite of the ones my mother would have made for me. I've molded myself physically, mentally, and spiritually into the kind of person Benji might be persuaded to love because I was too scared to figure out who I really was. I campaigned for and earned various roles within the Gilbert clan, roles that were not mine to claim, because I was desperate to feel as if I truly belonged somewhere, belonged to someone, even if at the core it was all artifice.

What a joke.

A bitter wind whips against the windows, rattling the glass, sending goose pimples across my bare flesh. And then I hear a loud pop and several small explosions, and through the sheer voile curtains I see fragments of Crayola-colored light smear across the sky.

Midnight.

I wasn't supposed to be here. I was supposed to be twirling in the arms of the boy who rescued me from my loneliness after the first white knight had been struck down. A boy I love, but with whom I can no longer be—at least not until I learn how to love myself, by myself.

Tonight, I am alone, and I am alone on purpose. Not because my father left me, or because my mother gave up on me, or because my pseudoboyfriend died on me.

I am alone because I need to be alone.

Or maybe I simply need to *be*.

ABOUT THE AUTHOR

Lara M. Zeises lives in Delaware, the Home of Tax-Free Shopping, where she grew up. She holds a Master of Fine Arts degree in creative writing from Emerson College. *Bringing Up the Bones* is her first novel. She can be reached at zeisgeist@aol.com.